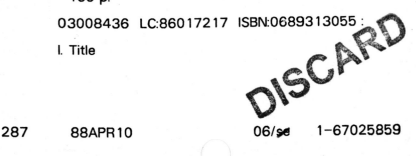

BOOKS BY BARBARA CORCORAN

A Dance to Still Music
The Long Journey
Meet Me at Tamerlaine's Tomb
A Row of Tigers
Sasha, My Friend
A Trick of Light
The Winds of Time
All the Summer Voices
The Clown
Don't Slam the Door When You Go
Sam
This Is a Recording
Axe-Time, Sword-Time
Cabin in the Sky
The Faraway Island
Make No Sound
Hey, That's My Soul You're Stomping On
"Me and You and a Dog Named Blue"
The Person in the Potting Shed
Rising Damp
You're Allegro Dead
A Watery Grave
August, Die She Must
The Woman in Your Life
Mystery on Ice
Face the Music
A Horse Named Sky
You Put Up With Me, I'll Put Up With You

You Put Up With Me, I'll Put Up With You

You Put Up With Me,

I'll Put Up With You

Barbara Corcoran

A JEAN KARL BOOK

Atheneum   1987   New York

Atheneum
Macmillan Publishing Company
866 Third Avenue, New York, NY 10022

Text set by Haddon Craftsmen, Allentown, Pennsylvania
Printed and bound by Fairfield Graphics, Fairfield, Pennsylvania
Designed by Marjorie Zaum
First Edition

10   9   8   7   6   5   4   3   2   1

Library of Congress Cataloging-in-Publication Data

Corcoran, Barbara.
You put up with me, I'll put up with you.

SUMMARY: Forced to move to a new town just as she thinks she
is finally starting to fit in with other young people,
twelve-year-old Kelly finds her feeling of alienation slowly
fading as she builds relationships with new family and friends.
[1. Interpersonal relations—Fiction] I. Title.
PZ7.C814Ym   1987   [Fic]   86-17217
ISBN 0-689-31305-5

This one is for Susan.

You Put Up With Me,
I'll Put Up With You

Chapter One

WHEN SHE THOUGHT ABOUT IT LATER, IT SEEMED TO Kelly that it had started out to be one of the best days of her life; but right at the end it turned into the absolute gruesome worst.

The good part began when Mrs. Halcom told her she was being cast as Mercutio in the school's spring production of Romeo and Juliet. It was Kelly's first year at this small private school in Wellesley, Massachusetts; and so far, instead of making the big splash she had hoped for, she had sunk without a trace. It is not easy to be totally inconspicuous in a seventh grade that has only twelve girls in it, but she had managed. The other girls had been in this school since the first grade, except for two who were "new kids," meaning they hadn't started until the fourth grade.

On many a night as she cried herself to sleep, she had said to her cat Angel, "You'd think I'd be all the more noticeable. I mean I'm new blood. I'm different. I'm from Boston. I went to a big public school. And you know good and well, Angel, I did all right. Straight A's, right? Except for math, of course. And I played the triangle in the orchestra. It wasn't symphony caliber, but I helped keep the rhythm. And I was Titania in Assembly. And I wrote for the school paper. So I'm not a total nerd, right? Wrong. In the eyes of the seventh grade at Buckmaster School, I am zilch, zed, minus one."

She hadn't told her mother how she felt, because after Kelly's dad died, her mom had troubles enough. She had a job at an insurance company that she hated. She had moved to Wellesley, commuting every day, just so Kelly could go to this super school and get into one of the good colleges. So Kelly couldn't tell her how gruesome the school really was. She couldn't tell her how she had invited kids over and they never came, how she was always the last one chosen for a team, how nobody made friends with her.

"They aren't rude," she told Angel. "Mrs. Halcom is big on rudeness; I mean she's against it. So they say hi and stuff like that, but it's like I'm from outer space. I'm the E.T. of Buckmaster, only I haven't got a little friend."

But now! Now everything would be different. She was going to play Mercutio, and they would see how good she was. She had been a hit when she played Titania in that scene they did for Assembly at her other school. "Highlights from Shakespeare," it had been called. Stage presence, that was what the school paper said she had. And charm. She had spent several weeks dreaming of a career in the theater.

Her mom wasn't home when Kelly got in from school. She never got home before six, and if the traffic was bad, it would be later.

So, Kelly told Angel her thrilling news. Angel was a middle-aged calico cat that her father had bought her when Kelly was seven, the year before he died. Angel sat on the sofa and thoughtfully washed her many-colored face while Kelly told her about the play.

"They'll have to notice me. You can't ignore Mercutio." She got her mother's umbrella from the closet and brandished it like a sword. "Think of the spangled tights! And the duels. 'Come, sir, your passado!' " She flourished the umbrella. "The death scene is tremendous. I read it today in study hall. 'I am hurt. A plague o' both your houses.' " She clutched her stomach. " 'I am sped!' " She aimed the sword at Angel, who yawned. "Come, Tybalt, en garde!"

Angel rolled on her back, all four feet in the air.

"It's not you who dies," Kelly said, "it's me. Your line is, 'What wouldst thou have with me?' And I say, 'Good king of cats, nothing but one of your nine lives; that I mean to make bold withal, and as you use hereafter, dry-beat the rest of the eight.' It really says that about king of cats. Get up and fight, Angel."

But Angel looked calmly at Kelly with no sign of fight in her green eyes.

Kelly collapsed on the sofa beside her. "Some dandy you are." She scratched Angel's ears. "After Mrs. Halcom announced the cast, Holly Ives walked out to the bus with me. Her mother was waiting in this Audi 5000. Holly Ives said, 'Hey, maybe you can come over some night and we'll practice dueling.' I was so excited, I broke out giggling. She gave me this amused look and said, 'Don't sweat it, MacArthur.' " Kelly pulled Angelica onto her lap. "So what did that mean? Is she going to be friends or what?"

Angel chewed the tip of Kelly's finger. Kelly turned on the TV, but she couldn't keep her mind on *Wheel of Fortune.* She was imagining herself taking curtain calls, and Holly Ives saying, "You were wonderful, Kelly. Let's be friends. You're really a very interesting person."

It was the first time in her life that Kelly had not made friends. She still saw her Boston friends now and then on special occasions when her mom and Jill's and Frannie's moms got together and planned a weekend, but they were all so busy, that didn't happen often; and her mom was not crazy about Kelly's taking the bus into Boston alone.

She was pretty sure it was not that they didn't like her at Buckmaster. They just had these set-in-concrete friendships and groups that were formed years ago.

She jumped up, upsetting Angel who rolled sideways with a protesting meow. Kelly could hardly wait to tell her mother about Mercutio. She went into the kitchen and put Mexican TV dinners in the oven. She washed some lettuce and sliced a couple of tomatoes.

The small apartment kitchen was hot, with late afternoon sun slanting in through the window. It had been a warm day for early May. Angel sprawled in a patch of sunshine, her hind legs stretched out behind her. Kelly opened a bottle of Classic Coke and sat on the stool beside the counter. She studied the snapshot of her father in its silver frame. Now that Grandma was dead too, she tried to picture all of them—her dad and his parents and the uncle who died before she was born—all of them together somewhere, Grandfather cracking jokes and Grandma saying, "Now, John," and laughing at the same time. Dad would upstage them all. Her Uncle Barry always stayed a shadowy figure in her imagination, like a ghost, although she had seen plenty of pictures of him in his Air Force uniform. In her mind he never said anything.

They would be in their real house on the river in Essex, where her dad and her grandmother had grown up, the house Kelly loved so much to visit. Her mother had inherited it, and some day it would probably be Kelly's. She liked to think about it—her safe place, her security. She hadn't been back there since Grandma's funeral.

She heard the special cough of the old Volvo as it came into the parking area behind the apartment house. Grabbing the umbrella again and putting on an old blue beret from her mother's hippie days, she posed like a fencer beside the door.

Her mother came in out of breath, jingling her keys. "Kelly? You home?" She jumped when Kelly darted out with sword at the ready. Then she laughed. "Kelly, wait till you hear! I've got the most terrific news."

"Me too," Kelly said.

But her mother told her news first, and that was when Kelly felt as if one of the best days of her life had turned into one of the most absolutely horrendous worst.

Chapter Two

"BUT HONEY," HER MOTHER SAID, "IT'S NOT AS IF YOU were Romeo. Mercutio dies in the middle of the play."

"You don't understand." Kelly felt terrible. She couldn't even work up a good crying fit. She was afraid it would look like an act.

Her mother sighed. "I guess I don't. I thought you hated that school."

"I never said that."

"No, because you didn't want to worry me; but you looked so grim every night, you didn't have to spell it out. I heard you crying after you went to bed. And when I asked you how school was going, you gritted your teeth and said 'okay.' I mean you were not in transports of joy, sweetie. I even called Mrs. Halcom . . ."

"You didn't!" What mothers would do! It was treachery.

". . . and she said she was sure you would start fitting in soon. Fitting in has never been your problem."

"Mercutio was going to be my toehold."

Her mother laughed and then said quickly, "I'm sorry."

Kelly's own tendency to laugh at the wrong time was inherited from her mother.

"Please listen again while I explain it. I really think you're going to love it."

"I'm not," Kelly said, "but you can explain it if you want to. It makes no sense to me." She thought she smelled the TV dinners. She ought to take them out of the oven, but at that point she didn't care if they burned to a crisp.

"You have heard a million times how your dad and I grew up in Essex . . ."

"And couldn't wait to leave."

"That was then. This is now. You know we kept in close touch with our crowd, the friends we went to school with."

Kelly had been hearing about the crowd all her life. She didn't feel she knew them all that well herself because whenever her parents took her to Essex, Kelly stayed with her grandmother while her parents visited their old friends. So Butch and Nanci and Ponty and Sarita and their kids were mostly just names.

Now her grandmother was dead, and Kelly didn't want to go to Essex yet. She was afraid the house would look different, and it would be too lonesome. But now her mother was telling her they were going to *live* there, and not only in the town but in her grandmother's house with Nanci and Sarita and ten thousand kids.

"You know your father and I talked for years about opening a restaurant."

"I thought it was just talk."

"I told you that Sarita and Nanci and I bought the old one-room schoolhouse, after Ponty left Sarita."

"I thought it was an investment."

"Well, it is, but we have to make it pay off. The carpenters and plumbers have been working on it all spring."

"Now you tell me."

"Kelly, I've talked about it before, but you never paid attention."

Kelly was silent. Her mother was probably right; she often didn't hear half of what she was told, because she had so much to tell herself.

"The place is a natural," her mother said, looking very eager. "Great location, right size, room for expansion . . ."

"You don't know how to run a restaurant."

Her mother sighed. "Kelly, all of us worked in Essex restaurants all through high school and college summers. We've bussed, waited on tables, shucked clams, and even cooked sometimes. And Sarita has been working as a waitress and a hostess ever since she and Ponty broke up."

Kelly knew all that too, but she hadn't thought it had anything to do with her. Now suddenly it had everything to do with her. "I suppose you'll lose all the money Grandma left you."

Her mother looked stern. "Your money is in trust if that's what's worrying you."

Kelly flushed. She wished she hadn't said that.

"We've all saved for this, and Butch is very supportive of Nanci's part in it. He's at sea so much it's almost as if he's never there, and he's glad Nanci will have some company. And of course we got a loan from the bank." She sighed again. "I thought this was going to delight you. I'll never understand kids."

"I hate it," Kelly said.

Her mother looked hurt. She went into the kitchen, and when she came back, she said, "The TV dinners are burned up. Where do you want to go to eat?"

"The Inn."

Kelly didn't want to act as though she were pleased to be going to the Inn, but she was. Their ice cream on meringues with hot fudge sauce were something she fantasized about.

"What about school?" she said when they were settled at their table in the Inn.

"There's not that much time before the end of the school term, and Buckmaster is ahead of the public schools anyway. You can go into the eighth grade in the fall, and you'll be ready for the Regional High School the next year. It's in Hamilton. Esther and Jake go there."

Esther. That was Sarita's daughter, about sixteen. Jake belonged to Nanci and Butch. Kelly hadn't seen him since they were little kids. He'd be fifteen or sixteen too, a terrible age for boys.

"How old are those little kids?"

"Jeannette is about five, and Alexander is eight or nine. Goodness, kids grow up fast. He was such an adorable baby."

Kelly shuddered. A little later, toying with her crabmeat cocktail, she said, "Mom . . ."

"Yes, dear?"

Kelly felt almost sorry for her mother, she looked so anxious. But she had gotten them into this, hadn't she?

"I am an only child, right?"

"Right."

"No siblings, right?"

"Right."

"And now you expect me to plunge into this huge mass of human beings—if you count five year olds as human—sharing my private life with two teenagers and two babies and ninety-nine grown women all of whom are practically strangers to me . . ." She paused as a dreadful thought struck her. "I'll have my own room, won't I?"

Her mother gave her attention to a wedge of tomato that she was trying to cut. "Well, actually, honey, the way we worked it out, we thought you and Esther could share the third floor. It's a huge room, you remember, practically the whole third floor, with your own bathroom and those great dormer windows looking out on the river, and two big closets. . . ."

Kelly put down her fork. "I can't believe it. I can't believe my own mother would do this to me."

"Kelly, you always loved that room."

"But not with *people* in it!" Her voice rose, and her mother frowned and shook her head. "I'd rather kill myself than share my room."

"Oh, don't be so dramatic."

"You're asking more than any human mother should ask of her child." Kelly swallowed hard. "I won't do it."

She knew she had gone too far. Her mother put down her fork very quietly and in the soft voice she used when she was really angry, she said, "That's enough. You're acting like a spoiled brat. I am trying to make a good life for us. I want to do something interesting for a change. I'm sick to death of insurance files. And I don't want to worry from month to month about paying the bills."

"We could live on Grandma's money."

"Not forever. Besides, I want to save some of that for you."

"I don't want it when I'm too old to enjoy it."

Her mother looked at her coldly. "I am ashamed of the way you are sounding."

Kelly knew when she was licked. At least for the time being. She ordered her ice cream-meringue-fudge-sauce and didn't say another word. She might as well enjoy the dessert even if the rest of her life was in shambles.

Neither of them mentioned Essex again, but later when Kelly was in bed crying into Angel's orange and black and white fur, her mother came in and sat on the bed.

"I'm really sorry you're so upset," she said. "I guess I didn't realize you'd take it this way. You used to be a good sport about new adventures. But I suppose there comes an age . . ." She paused for a minute. "I do think I'm doing the right thing. Mercutio or no Mercutio you were not happy at that school. I think it will do you good to have other family to adjust to. Being an only child is a lonely business."

Now she tells me. "What if the restaurant fails?" She cheered up a little at the thought.

In a firm voice her mother said, "It is not going to fail." She kissed Kelly's forehead and said good-night.

"Well," Kelly said to Angel, "we can hope, can't we? Maybe I can think of something. For her own good, of course."

Chapter Three

THE OLD VOLVO WAGON WAS PILED HIGH WITH ALL THE things they hadn't let the mover take in case he might break or lose them: Kelly's record albums and tapes, a lot of her books, the teddy bear Alfonse that she'd had since she was four, her mother's Spode tea set, the pictures of Kelly's dad, and the ancestral teaspoons. Lying nonchalantly across the top of everything was Angel.

Kelly felt her stomach lurch as her mother turned onto Route 97. She hadn't been to Essex since her grandmother's funeral. She had gone on imagining the house just as it was, but now it would be changed and awful.

The countryside looked lush and green after the

spring rains, and lilacs were blooming everywhere. Trees and bushes were thicker, somehow, than they were south of Boston, and greener, something like, she imagined, what a rain forest would be. Wisteria hung over the porches of some of the houses, and the houses themselves were different here, older, some of them dating back to the seventeenth century.

They turned off 1-A onto Rubbly Road.

"I love the street names in Essex County," her mother said. She had been trying to make conversation ever since Boston.

"Like what?"

"Oh, Labor-in-Vain Road in Ipswich, and Downfall Road and West Ox Pasture and Way to the River. They're the old names from the days of the settlers. Wenham used to be called Enon, they say, because someone discovered it was unmapped, so they called it NONE spelled backwards."

Kelly laughed, although she didn't mean to. "Are you making it up?"

"No."

Soon they were coming into Essex. Kelly saw the stream where her granddad used to take her to see the alewives run every year. Then they were passing the big town hall. She couldn't help being a little excited, but it was spoiled when she thought about how things were going to be.

Her mother slowed down near the Causeway, where cars were heading into town for fried clams and shore dinners. The Causeway crossed a turn in the salt water river; where once there had been shipyards, now there were restaurants and a marina. Boats were coming upriver with the tide, sports fishermen looking sunburned and happy. "Like Hemingway characters," her dad used to say. Gulls flew close to the sterns of the boats looking for handouts.

"Will we have a boat?" Kelly asked.

"Maybe, some day. Sarita has a dory."

Kelly had in mind a sailboat or one of those fancy inboards, not a broken-down old dory.

"There's the schoolhouse!" Her mother slowed down, looking excited.

Kelly had seen the empty old schoolhouse a hundred times. The only difference now, as far as she could see, was the plumber's truck in the yard, and an addition built onto the back that wasn't painted yet. Big deal. Who would want to eat in a stupid old schoolhouse?

As they got closer to her grandmother's house, Kelly clenched her hands so hard that they ached. She kept remembering Grandma's funeral, and thinking how different it was all going to be.

And then there they were, in the driveway of the big square house with the dormer windows on the third floor. The third floor she was going to have to share with somebody named Esther. She felt sick.

She did a double take. "They've painted the house!" Instead of the nice weathered gray, it was so white it made your eyes smart. And the door was blue. Nobody had a blue door! Two big planters were on either side of the steps, full of bright red geraniums. Grandmother had not liked red geraniums. "Too flashy," she always said.

"Red, white, and blue," Kelly muttered. "Looks like a flag."

Her mother acted as if she hadn't heard her. "Doesn't the house look nice? Nanci and Sarita did it themselves. Isn't it fantastic?"

"Fantastic is the word," Kelly said.

"Kelly," her mother said sharply.

As they came up the wide stone steps, the blue door flew open and suddenly there was what seemed to Kelly a mob scene. Cast of thousands.

She was hugged, she was kissed, she was exclaimed over, as if she were the first person in history to have grown a few inches between the ages of eight and twelve. What did they expect—a midget?

The dark little woman with white paint streaks on her cutoffs was Nanci. The hearty blonde with the loud voice was Sarita, who never stopped talking and laughing. Kids lurked.

Alexander made a dramatic entrance, sliding down Kelly's grandmother's bannister, something Kelly had never been allowed to do, tempting though it was. Alexander had a round, serious face, and glasses. He stared at Kelly as if she were a rare creature in a zoo. She wished she could squirt a mouthful of water at him, the way the macaque monkey had done to her at Franklin Park zoo.

"Alexander, how you've grown," her mother said. She made a half-hearted grab at hugging, which he managed to escape without seeming rude. Kelly had to give him credit for that. Ducking hugs gracefully was an art.

"Honey," his mother Sarita said to him, "help bring in the bags." And to Kelly she said, "Esther and Jake will be home from school any minute now. Esther can't wait to see you."

I'll bet, Kelly thought, but she smiled politely. Not for nothing a year under the eagle eye of Mrs. Halcom. She could fake it with the best of them. She noticed that nothing was said about Jake's dying to see her. He would probably turn out to be the biggest pain of all. Her experience with boys between the ages of fourteen and sixteen had prepared her for the worst. Their idea of a real laugh was to trip you up and scream with hilarity. Either that or ignore you totally.

The movers had arrived before them, and some of the familiar furniture still stood in the middle of the living room waiting for her mother's instructions. The house, big as it was, looked crowded. Too many people's things had been moved in, and some of her grandmother's things had disappeared altogether. Where was the rocking chair she always sat in by the bay window? Where was her little mahogany sewing cabinet? Nothing looked right.

Jeannette was still rubbing her eyes after her nap. At least Kelly supposed it was Jeannette, unless they'd rung another kindergartner in on her. The child stared at Kelly suspiciously.

"This is your new sister, Kelly," Sarita told her.

"My sister's Esther," Jeannette said.

Sarita had already turned away, chattering to Kelly's mother.

Kelly returned Jeannette's stare. She wanted to say, "I don't like it any better than you do, kid."

"Kelly, let's get our things upstairs, dear," her mother said. "You know where your room is."

"You mean Esther's room and mine," Kelly said carefully.

Her mother gave her a look. Kelly grabbed two suitcases and started upstairs. Jeannette, thumb in mouth, followed her. Alexander came tearing downstairs again and nearly ran into her.

"We need traffic lights here," Kelly said.

Surprisingly, Alexander laughed.

It had never seemed like a very long way up to the third floor when she was visiting, but today she felt as if she were climbing a mountain. The suitcases seemed ten times as heavy as they had at home. At home. She *was* at home. Yuk. It was like moving into a subway station at rush hour.

In the past she had loved the big airy room that had been made by walling off half the attic. It had casement windows and bright-colored rugs that her

Grandmother had braided. Once it had had a huge four poster bed; but as soon as Kelly opened the door, she saw that that was gone.

The room looked as though someone had laid a plumb line down the middle. On one side there was a stripped single bed with clean sheets and an afghan folded at the bottom; a chest of drawers, a small desk, and a combination table-bookcase. That half of the room was as empty as a hospital room.

In the other half, a single bed had a quilt pulled up over a jumble of sheets. Two sweaters, jeans, a wrinkled blouse and some shorts were thrown on the bed. A Sweet Dreams paperback lay face down and open on the pillow.

The bureau was loaded with makeup, plastic curlers, a comb and brush, a hand mirror, a ukulele with broken strings, a cheerleader's pompon, and three snapshots of the same boy. The desk was littered with papers, notebooks, school books, pens with the caps left off, letters out of their envelopes, and a looseleaf journal.

Kelly sat down on her bed. She had a pack rat for a roommate. She felt too depressed to cry. Jeannette stood in the doorway, watching her.

"Thanks for seeing me to my room," Kelly said. "Goodbye."

The child didn't move.

Kelly tried to ignore her. If she got a screen to divide the room in half, that might help. It wouldn't be real privacy, but it would be better than this. She'd demand a screen. Or else. Or else what? It was hopeless. No minority was so persecuted as children. People were always telling you to grow up . . . "you're almost thirteen, Kelly" . . . but she knew it wouldn't be one bit different. Maybe she would write to her congressman. Jefferson and Lincoln and those guys never said you were only free if you were over eighteen. It was a blot on America's escutcheon. She began to frame a letter in her mind. "Dear Congressman . . . Congress-person?"

Somebody was running up the stairs with a lot of clumping and thumping. Jeannette was galvanized into life. She whirled around and shouted, "She's here, she's here."

A large, blonde, breathless girl stood in the doorway smiling. "Hi," she said, "I'm Esther."

Kelly half expected her to produce a menu. She sounded like those waitresses that tell you their name and expect you to beam at them. "Hi," she said. "I'm Kelly."

Esther giggled. "I know that." She was tall for her age and well-developed.

I am never going to be well-developed, Kelly thought. I'll do exercises so it won't happen. It's gross.

Esther had blonde curly hair, rumpled as if she'd been in a high wind. Her cheeks were red and tanned like a peach. She had pale blue eyes and eyebrows haphazardly made up. Although she was standing in one place she seemed to give off energy. Restless types made Kelly nervous.

Nobody spoke for a long minute, and Esther's smile began to look strained. Kelly realized she was probably looking hostile, so she tried to rearrange her face. She ought to say something.

"Well, here we are," she said, and in spite of her good intentions, she just barely kept from groaning.

"Isn't it great?" Esther beamed again and bounced over to her bed, swept the clothes onto the floor and sat down. "I love this room, don't you? The view is neat. At our house I had a room half this big and I had to share it with Jeannette."

"Barf," Jeannette said. She stood in the doorway watching them.

Esther made a face. "Bug off, Jeannette." To Kelly she said, "Aren't little sisters a pain?"

"I wouldn't know," Kelly said.

"Oh, that's right." Esther looked as if she had made a terrible blunder, pointing out some handicap. "I forgot you're an only child. That must be hard."

Kelly took a deep breath. "It depends on your point of view." She looked at Jeannette, who put her thumb in her mouth and stared back. "I have to un-pack now."

"I'll help," Esther said.

"No, thanks. I can do it."

While Kelly unpacked, Esther talked and talked.

At the end of half an hour Kelly knew that her grade average was B-, her favorite teacher was Mr. Prescott who taught history and had big brown eyes, her boyfriend was named Peter, and for years she had been practicing for and dreaming of the day she would make the pep squad. "I spent a month at cheerleading camp last summer," she said. "It was fabulous. Some really cute boys."

"I didn't know boys were cheerleaders."

"Oh, yes. It's a real art now, you know. I practice every day."

Kelly had always thought cheerleaders were demented, but she tried to smile politely. She wished her mother could see how patient and good she was being under great stress.

Esther switched to music. Her favorite rock band was The Talking Heads, her favorite singer was Madonna, her favorite bus driver was Herman who could whistle through his teeth, and her absolutely favorite-to-die color was burnt orange.

Kelly felt exhausted. Esther seemed to use up all the oxygen in the room. She hung up her last blouse and flopped onto her bed. "I'm going to take a nap," she said. "I have a headache."

Esther looked incredulous. "You take naps? You're not sick, are you?"

"I am not sick."

Esther looked suddenly deflated. "Well, I guess I'll go downstairs. I don't want to bother you."

Kelly felt a pang of guilt. "That's okay," she said, not specifying what was okay.

"I talk too much," Esther said.

Kelly gritted her teeth and said, "It was very interesting."

Esther gave her a troubled look. "Come on, Jeannette. Kelly wants to rest."

"She's sick," Jeannette said in a loud voice. "I'll get her some pills."

"I am not sick." Kelly raised her voice slightly.

"She's going to throw up," Jeannette said, as Esther dragged her from the room. "I want to show her how I gargle."

"No!" Esther said. There was a sound of thumping, as if Esther was hauling her sister down the stairs.

Loudly Jeannette said, "But I've just learned. I want to show her."

Kelly pulled the pillow over her face. This was her new home.

Suddenly she remembered Angel. Where was her cat? She sat up. How could she have forgotten? Somewhere in this vast, people-ridden house, poor Angel was lost and alone. Anything could happen to her. She leaped off the bed and ran downstairs.

Angel was sitting on a window seat purring as Jeannette patted her back and said, "Nice kitty. You're going to be my nice kitty."

Slowly Kelly went back upstairs. Even Angel had deserted her.

Chapter Four

KELLY DIDN'T WANT TO ADMIT THAT SHE WAS HUNGRY, but the smells of cooking coming up the stairs were almost too good to bear. She had thought of skipping dinner, saying she was not hungry, maybe impressing them all with her spiritual quality, but that aroma . . . was it roast lamb? . . . banished the notion from her mind. She got up, washed her face and changed her shirt. No one had come near her, and she felt as if she were an invalid with a communicable disease. Not even her mother had come, not even Angel. Relationships were certainly undependable.

Cautiously she opened the door and started down the two flights of stairs. On the second flight, there was a clatter behind her, and before she could even turn around, Alexander tore past her. He was wearing cowboy boots and spurs. *Spurs?*

"Chow time," he yelled at her over his shoulder.

This was a child who obviously spent most of his life charging up and down stairs, a very unnerving habit.

Jeannette was sitting on a scrofulous-looking rocking horse at the foot of the stairs. Rocking monotonously back and forth, she watched Kelly come down.

A disembodied voice that had to be Sarita's called out, "Jeannette! Go wash up for supper. I told you before."

Jeannette paid no attention.

Kelly wandered into the big living room. For a moment she thought no one was there, but then she saw Angel, rising up from the brick hearth in front of the fireplace and luxuriously stretching. Angel came over to her, swinging her hips in that unflappable way cats have.

"Traitor," Kelly said to her.

Angel made a flying leap and settled herself on Kelly's shoulder, purring contentedly. In spite of herself Kelly was glad to see her.

"Oh, there you are, dear." It was Sarita, bustling into the room with an apron on, her face flushed. "Did you have a good rest? Esther said you were feeling a little under the weather."

"I'm fine," Kelly said quickly. Holly Ives had told

her that when a woman said she was under the weather, it meant she was having her period. She felt herself blush. "I just had a slight headache." And to change the subject she said, "Can I help with dinner?"

"No, thanks, honey, it's all under control. Why don't you come on into the dining room, and we'll get this show on the road."

Sarita was certainly a hearty type. Kelly followed her to the dining room, where Nanci was setting out the silver on Kelly's grandmother's table with the leaves in it, the way they used to be for Christmas dinner when Grandfather and Grandmother and Kelly's dad were alive.

Nanci smiled at her. "You could fill the milk glasses for the children," she said. "Sarita's three sit on this side, and we've put you over there next to your mother. Did you have a good rest?"

Kelly wondered if Esther had also given a news story to the local paper: KELLY MacARTHUR COLLAPSES FROM FATIGUE AND TAKES NAP. She went into the kitchen for the milk, and found her mother making the salad. They were all acting as if this were some kind of party, Sarita humming along with a golden oldie on the radio, Nanci smiling as if it were Christmas, her own mother looking relaxed and pleased.

Esther came barreling in the back door in a lavender jumpsuit. She had obviously been jogging, because she jogged in place in the kitchen, as if she were wound up and couldn't quit till the motor ran down. Her cheeks were pink.

"Hi," Esther said, enthusiastically. "Did you have a good . . ."

"Yes, thank you," Kelly said before she could finish. "Did you . . . uh . . . have a jolly jog?"

Esther laughed, but Kelly caught the warning look her mother threw at her. Her mother knew when she was being sarcastic, and she had said quite often that it was not one of Kelly's most charming traits.

After some calling and confusion, they were all assembled at the dining room table.

Kelly looked around. It didn't even look like her grandmother's table, except that there was the same burned place where someone had put down a hot dish long ago. "Where's Jake?"

Esther answered. "Jake has a paper route. He eats by himself when he gets home. He has a room upstairs over the stable. Isn't that weird?"

"Oh, the lucky duck," Kelly said. Everyone looked at her, and her mother was frowning.

"I mean," Kelly said hastily, "it must be fun to have a tiny little place of your own. So quiet and peaceful and everything." She knew she was babbling.

"Well, I think it's weird," Esther said. "He could have shared that nice big room Alexander has."

Alexander stopped his concentrated eating long enough to say, "It is not weird. It's cool. He's fixed it up real great. He's got a stereo and his guitar; and if he doesn't make his bed, nobody even knows it."

Kelly remembered that room in the barn. It had been a hayloft once, and then Grandmother had had it fixed up so the hired man could live there and take care of things after Grandfather died. She ached with envy. Why hadn't she thought to claim it, before the odious Jake had? Not that she knew him, but he had to be odious. All boys that age were. If he played the guitar, he probably had a punk haircut and never washed it, and dirty jeans, and sneakers with the laces missing. Yuk.

But she had to admit it was a good dinner, just the kind of meal she liked: roast lamb with mint jelly, scalloped potatoes, lima beans, and her mother's salad with the garlic dressing. The conversation went on all around her, like waves breaking on the beach. Her mother and Sarita were talking about the best places to get restaurant supplies, and Esther was telling Nanci in great detail about her pep squad practice. Jeannette sometimes stopped shoveling food into her mouth long enough to say something irrelevant, like, "Kelly's cat likes me best." Alexander ate in silence, as if he was convinced he might never get another meal.

Dessert, which was Indian pudding with vanilla ice cream on top, went on for a long time, because the mothers dawdled over their coffee and discussed old classmates. Kelly itched to be excused, but she thought it was not wise to be the first. She was already in trouble with her mother, she was pretty sure.

Finally Alexander finished his second helping of pudding, wiped his mouth with the back of his hand, said, " 'Scuse me," and bolted from the room. A carrot stuck out of his pocket.

"I'll clear the table," Kelly said, seizing the opportunity.

"I'll wash," Esther said. Esther seemed in no hurry to get up. She was actually enjoying all the small town gossip.

Weird, Kelly thought, stacking some dishes and pushing open the swinging door into the kitchen. She almost dropped the dishes when she saw that she was not alone in the room. Though it was silly, she decided afterwards, never to expect to find myself alone in this house. A tall, dark, quite handsome boy was sitting at the kitchen table, eating from a piled-up plate of meat and potatoes. He glanced up, gave her a slight nod, and went back to his food.

It took Kelly a moment to realize that this was Jake. She put the dishes down beside the sink. "Hi," she said.

"Hi." He had a deep voice. After one quick look he went on eating.

She felt a little strange, almost shy. She hadn't expected him to be like this, so good-looking, so sort of grown-up. She stacked the dishes in the sink. "I guess you're Jake." Her voice sounded hoarse. She cleared her throat and choked. She leaned over the sink, trying to stop the strangling sounds coming out of her mouth. After a moment she heard his chair pushed back, and then felt a thump between her shoulders. He poured half a glass of water and handed it to her.

She tried to drink it, but she was still choking. The water drooled out of the side of her mouth. She had never felt so humiliated in her life. Her eyes streamed. She wished she could fill the sink with water and put her head in it and not come up till he left.

He handed her a paper towel and went back to his dinner.

Gasping, she finally got hold of herself. She mopped her face, making a long job of it because she didn't want to turn around and face him. But she couldn't hang over the sink for the rest of her life. She took a breath, coughed, and turned around. "I was going to say," she said, speaking carefully so she wouldn't start choking again, "I'm Kelly."

He laughed, not a mean laugh, she decided later, but a sympathetic laugh, or at least a nice laugh.

"I figured," he said. He got up, rinsed off his plate and added it to the dirty dishes. "See ya."

He was gone. She stood there, dazed. Why did she feel so peculiar? She had seen plenty of good-looking boys before, without reacting like this. What was so great about Jake? Nothing, she told herself firmly; she had just happened to come upon him at an emotional moment in her life. She looked in the small mirror over the sink. Her face was red, her eyes looked as if she had been crying for days. Well, Kelly, she told herself, that was a great entrance.

She went out the back door, needing some air; it was claustrophobic with all those people filling up the house. She walked past the barn, in the direction of the house next door. Vaguely she remembered the kid who lived in that house, a scrawny, homely little kid who used to pester her. What was her name? Rosa? No, Rhonda. Grandmother had said to be nice to Rhonda because they were a deserving family. Kelly had never been sure what it was they deserved, but she had never made much of an effort to be nice. If you paid attention to kids like that, you had a friend for life, and that was not what she wanted; at least she didn't want Rhonda as a friend for life. Somebody like Holly Ives now, that would have been different.

She wondered if there would be anyone like Holly Ives at that school she had to go to in the fall. It seemed unlikely. They'd probably all turn out to be Rhondas.

She heard a sound from somewhere near the back of the house, and looked in that direction. There was the hint of a shadow, but then it was gone. Maybe just Mom or Sarita throwing out the garbage. Or Esther, only Esther took up more space, in every sense of the word. Kelly thought about years and years of sharing a room with Esther, and she didn't think she could bear it. Tears stung her eyes, and she rubbed them away fiercely. Crying was a baby way to handle things, and babies had no control over their lives. Well, at the moment neither did she.

She leaned against the sagging fence that separated Grandma's property from the house next door, and breathed deeply of the salty, fishy air. It was a good smell, although ordinarily you wouldn't think "fishy" was one of your gourmet aromas. She thought about the ocean, beyond the marshes, not visible from her except as a kind of difference in the horizon. If she were a boy and a couple of years older, she could ship out on a fishing boat and have a free, adventurous life, sailing to Nova Scotia and all those exciting places.

"Kelly, is that you?" It was a hoarse whisper, so close to her that she jumped.

"Who's there?" She strained her eyes to make out the shadowy figure on the other side of the fence.

The figure bounded up to the fence, a tall thin person in a long uneven skirt, a blouse that was too big and had rhinestones or something sewn all over it. The face thrust toward her was long and bony and freckled in big splotches, and the haircut was punk, partly a kind of reddish pink, partly jet black, spiking off in a dozen different directions. The eyes behind the granny glasses were bright.

"It's me—Rhonda." She was speaking in a loud whisper.

"Rhonda?" Kelly stared at her, trying to see the little kid she remembered in this tall, gawky girl with the outlandish clothes. She and Rhonda were the same age. "Is that really you, Rhonda?" She was whispering, too.

35

"Yes!" For real. Here, pinch me." Rhonda thrust out an arm encircled with four gaudy bracelets.

"Okay, I believe you." Aloud she said, "Why are we whispering?"

"Well, you just never know," Rhonda said mysteriously. "I'm so glad you're finally here. I've been watching and watching for you."

"You have?" Kelly felt a pang of dismay, at the same time realizing that here was a known person who was *not* living under the same roof with her. It suddenly seemed as if Rhonda really was an old buddy.

"Of course I have. We've got years to catch up on. And I'll show you the ropes."

"What ropes?"

"You know, the ropes. Who's having a passionate romance with who, and who's cheating on his girl friend, and where the real dishes are."

"Dishes?" Kelly began to feel as though she had wandered into a place where another language was spoken.

"Dishes. The dreamboats." With her other hand she made an arcing gesture toward the barn. "Like that one. The dream man of the world."

Kelly looked back at the barn.

"Jacob Childs DeWitt."

"Jake?" Well, Jake was handsome, all right, enough to make her choke on her own breath, but she wouldn't go so far as to say . . . "Rhonda, you're crazy."

Rhonda drew herself up another half inch and wrapped her long arms around herself. "Oh, no, I always knew when I saw HIM, I'd know it. When my dream man walked into my life, there'd be thunder in my ears and lightning in the sky. He did, and it did."

"But you've known Jake all your life."

"Kelly, there comes a time in a woman's life when she puts away childish things and faces her own new, real, passionate self . . ."

"Did you read that somewhere or did you make it up?"

"I read it in *When Passion Strikes*. It's the best book I've read in months. I'll lend it to you. It's *us*, Kelly."

"Not me," Kelly said firmly. "Well, it's nice seeing you again, Rhonda, but I guess I'd better go in."

In a low, mysterious voice Rhonda said, "Tomorrow night, same place, same time. Wear shoes you can walk in."

"Why?"

"You'll see." Rhonda sang the words. She glanced toward the road and suddenly stiffened. "Look!" she said, grabbing Kelly's wrist. "There it goes again!"

Kelly didn't want to encourage Rhonda by looking, but curiosity overcame her. "I don't see anything."

"There!" Rhonda's voice thrilled with suspense so convincing that Kelly felt a shiver in spite of herself.

She looked where Rhonda was pointing. Scuttling

along the side of the road, avoiding the streetlights, was . . . What? A strange, small, misshapen creature that looked more like a dark blob than a human being. As Kelly stared at it, it disappeared in the shadows, heading toward the river.

"What is it?" Kelly felt scared, and it made her mad. She didn't want to be scared by somebody like Rhonda, who never had good sense. But there *was* something; she had seen it with her own eyes.

"That's what we're going to find out," Rhonda said. "Remember, tomorrow night, same time, same place." She raised her arm high, her full sleeve dropping in a shadowy half circle away from her arm. "Till then, Peace." She scuttled toward her house in a bent-over shuffling run that reminded Kelly of a startled hen.

Kelly walked back to her house, trying not to hurry. The shadows all around her seemed to move. Rhonda was crazy as a bedbug, as her grandfather used to say, but there *had* been something eerie out there on the road.

Chapter Five

KELLY DIDN'T GO BACK THE NEXT NIGHT OR THE NIGHTS beyond that. When she thought about it in the reasonable light of day, it seemed just plain silly. Rhonda was in the local school all day, and Esther and Jake took off early for the Regional, so it was easy for Kelly to spend her days by herself. Even Jeannette was in nursery school or whatever it was.

Her mother suggested she help them at the schoolhouse-restaurant but Kelly stayed away. She explored her favorite places along the river, watched the clammers wading around at low tide with their hip boots and their three-pronged forks. It made her back ache to see them. When she mentioned it at dinner, Sarita said, "They say around here to be a clammer

39

you have to have a strong back and a weak mind."

It was curiosity that finally drew Kelly to the schoolhouse one day. At dinner the night before, all the talk had been about the new kitchen appliances that had arrived, the enormous refrigerator, the freezer, the big stove. She had never heard a bunch of women get so excited about dumb things like stoves and refrigerators. So she decided to take a look.

Her mother seemed pleased when she dropped in, as casually as she could, to see what was going on. She rumpled Kelly's hair and said, "It's about time! Curiosity killed the cat, right?"

"Satisfaction brought him back," Kelly said, and her mother laughed. She acted as if she had just won a point, but Kelly wasn't giving up any points yet.

She had to admit, though, that the changes in the old schoolhouse were impressive. The big added-on kitchen sparkled with white paint, and the appliances were certainly big. Outside, Sarita was painting the clapboards. She waved her paint brush at Kelly, showering the new window panes with tiny drops of paint.

"Oh, blast!" she said. "Look what I did."

"I'll get it." Kelly found a rag and went outside to wipe off the paint drops.

The man who had done the rewiring was there to make a final check. He grinned at Kelly. "Hi. I'm Albert Vance. Second cousin to your dad. How you doin'?"

"Fine, thank you." Kelly looked at his freckled

face trying to find some resemblance to her father. She had never lived anywhere where everybody knew everybody else, and most of them seemed to be related.

"I was in school with your Uncle Barry. Full of jokes, Barry was."

"He was?" Kelly was interested, but Mr. Vance disappeared, like Alice in Wonderland, down a hole beside the foundation. She had never thought of the ghost of Uncle Barry as making jokes. She always thought of him plunging into the sea in a flaming fighter plane, and everybody's grief afterward. She liked the idea of a jokey uncle.

"Have you seen the rest rooms?" Sarita said. "They're a joy to behold. Those kids who went to school here in the twenties and thirties would be amazed."

Kelly inspected the rest rooms. They were small but about as attractive as rest rooms could be. The ladies' room had a place to sit and gaze into the mirror, which Kelly did for a minute, wondering if she looked like Uncle Barry.

Her mother and Nanci were hard at work, her mom trying to handle the machine that was sanding the floors. Kelly took it away from her and worked carefully and thoroughly over the wide old boards that in some places were worn into shallow depressions by generations of children's feet. She tried to imagine those kids, slaving away at spelling and geography and all that stuff.

"You're a good worker, Kel," Nanci said, nodding approvingly at the floor with its layer of dust. "It's going to look great when we get the varnish on."

Kelly felt noble. Here she was, working hard, getting blisters on her hands, helping them get ready for a project she didn't even believe in. That had to be pretty unselfish.

She washed her hands in the pale blue washbasin in the ladies' room, being careful to leave it clean. If Esther were doing this, she'd probably leave a mess.

She joined the three women, sitting on the floor and drinking Cokes. They all seemed tired, but they were still enthusiastic.

"We can get Henry Moses to take that big old stove," Sarita said, nodding toward the fat iron stove that had once heated the school room. "And what do we do with the blackboard? Cover it or take it out or what?"

Kelly looked around the room. "If you're going to call this place The School House, why don't you leave it like that?"

They all looked at her.

"Like what, honey?" her mother said.

"Like a school. Use the blackboard to write the menu every day. That way you save on printed menus. And you could get one of those big geography maps for the other part. That stove is nice. It looks cozy."

Sarita clapped her hands. "Kelly, you're a genius! That's a wonderful idea about the stove. We can have a trailing plant on top . . ."

"But the stove is so big. It would make room for another table," Nanci said.

"Do you want picturesque or do you want picturesque?" Kelly said. She was feeling quite pleased with herself. You didn't get called a genius every day.

"I think Kelly's right," her mother said slowly. "Why didn't we think of that?"

"Okay, the blackboard and stove stay," Sarita said. "That's two jobs we don't have to do. Now let's talk cuisine . . ."

Kelly interrupted. She was an authority on schoolhouse-restaurants now. "You don't talk cuisine when you've got an old schoolhouse. You talk *food.*"

"Kelly," her mother began.

"Let her speak," Sarita said. "She has good ideas."

Kelly tried not to look smug. "This is supposed to be a plain old fashioned place, right? So you need plain food, but different, extra good, okay? Like . . ." She stopped to think. They were listening. "Mom, remember that place Dad used to take us sometimes, called the Blue Something?"

"Blue Strawberry." Her mother exchanged a smile with Sarita and Nanci.

The smile looked as if they were saying, "Isn't she a bright little girl?" the way her third grade teacher used to say it to her mother; but they must be smiling for a different reason because they were listening, and they were paying attention to her ideas.

"They had just one kind of food each day, and

you had to take it or leave it, but it was always good. Remember?"

"We remember," Nanci said.

"You could have . . . like . . . that good fish chowder Grandma made on Mondays. On Tuesdays . . ." She frowned, thinking. "Broiled swordfish but no dumb sauces." She was naming her own favorite foods.

"It's a wonderful idea." Nanci finished her Coke and gathered up the empty cans. "We're so glad you've pitched in with us, Kelly."

"One big happy family," Sarita said. "I wonder if we'll ever get the smell of wet rubbers out of this place." She grabbed a mop and went at one of the corners.

Kelly wished they had gone on listening to her wonderful ideas, but suddenly they were all busy again. She began to sweep up the mess that the sander had made. She thought about the tingle of excitement she had felt when she gave them her suggestions. It made her feel good. It wasn't that she approved of this project, or that she found living here any more bearable than it had been. It was just that a person liked to have her ideas appreciated.

The school bus rolled up across the road with its usual squeak and rattle and gasp of air brakes, and a moment later Esther burst in, her book pack bouncing on her broad shoulders.

As usual Esther's entrance seemed to create a

disturbance of air, the way a tornado would. "Hey, everybody," Esther was saying. "Guess what! I got a B in the chem test and that clears me, marks-wise, for the pep squad tryouts. How about that!" She aimed a friendly punch at Kelly's biceps and missed as Kelly ducked. "You all have to come. It's going to be open to the public. It'll be terrific!" She twirled up and down the room, almost tripping over Kelly's broom.

Kelly watched appraisingly. Every day she found Esther harder to take. It was all that good cheer and enthusiasm and bounciness that got to her, and the mess she always left in her half of the room, and the way she talked on and on about boy friends and her "gang" and her blasted cheerleading when Kelly wanted to go to sleep.

"It's quitting time," Nanci said. "Let's knock off for today. We can have a meeting after supper and follow up Kelly's plan."

"*Kelly's* plan?" Esther looked suspicious.

"Kelly had a wonderful idea for the restaurant," Sarita said. "We'll tell you later."

They bustled around putting away mops and cleaning cloths and the paint brush Sarita had been using on the window frames.

"I'll clean the brush," Kelly said, getting herself a smile of approval from her mother. "I'll lock up." Actually she wanted some time to herself to think. She realized that her goals were in conflict, and she needed to do some serious thinking. She definitely did not

45

want this place to open, or if it did open, she did not want it to be a success. Because when it failed, the group would drift apart. They would have to find other things to do, and she and her mother would have the house to themselves, and she would have some privacy again.

When they had all gone, she cleaned the paint brushes and then sat down on the raised hearth of the big potbellied stove. They should definitely leave the stove the way it is, she thought, just polish it up and leave it. She couldn't believe that these women, who thought they were going to run a successful restaurant, actually had so few good ideas.

But there I go again, she told herself, thinking of ways to make it work. If she kept her mouth shut, it would flop. So she would keep her mouth shut. She leaned back against the hard, cold iron of the stove and closed her eyes. Her muscles ached from all the reaching, and running that heavy sander on the floor hadn't been any cinch. Let Esther try it; and that awful little Jeannette, always hanging around, spying on her. Then she'd run all over the house chanting things like, "Kelly's tweezing her eyebrows, ha, ha, ha." It was the first time in her entire life that Kelly had removed so much as one single hair from her thick brows; but she had seen Jake glance at them and knew what he was thinking: He was thinking, 'Why doesn't that girl trim her eyebrows? She looks like an orangutan or something.' Not that he'd say so. Not that he ever said anything except "Hi," or "How ya," or "Yep." She hardly ever saw him. When he wasn't in school or on his paper route, he usually sat up in his room in the barn playing his guitar. She couldn't hear him from the house, but sometimes she hung around the barn where he couldn't see her. He was really good at the guitar, and sometimes his friends came by with a banjo and a fiddle. They sounded great together, really professional.

She had to be careful not to be seen by Rhonda though. Several times she'd seen Rhonda hanging over the fence waiting for a glimpse of Jake. Kelly herself would never say that she was falling in love with Jake; she didn't use that kind of language. That was Rhonda's kind of language. But every now and then when she was in the drugstore, she sneaked a look at one of those romances; they said if your heart pounded and you felt all hot and weird and couldn't think of anything to say in the presence of the Significant Other, those were signs.

She closed her eyes and thought about living alone in her grandmother's house with nobody around but Jake. She'd fix up the barn into a better place for her mother, a real apartment. And she'd take over grandmother's bedroom and have peace and privacy at last. She frowned and opened her eyes. If she was married, she'd have to share the room. She wouldn't have any privacy at all. Of course it would be Jake, but . . . She shook her shoulders. She wasn't going to think about any of that stuff like her mother had tried to tell her about Life and Marriage. It was bad enough when Mrs. Halcom had held that class in Life Experience, and told them all those revolting things. She'd been so embarrassed, she could hardly stay in her seat. Holly Ives had giggled, and Mrs. Halcom had been mad. "Holly," she'd said, "this is not funny. This is very serious business. Happy married love is your key to mental health and happiness . . ." Well, if that was the key, Kelly preferred to leave the door locked. She did not want to grow up; everything about it seemed gross. Maybe if you concentrated, you could avoid growing up ever. Of course you'd get bigger and look older and some day you'd get gray hair and wrinkles and all, but you could stay ungrownup in your own head if you really wanted to. At least she thought she could, and she was certainly going to try.

She came out of the schoolhouse backwards, trying to avoid the wet paint around the door frame. She had the key in the lock and was about to turn it when a voice behind her startled her.

"You!" It was a hoarse, asthmatic kind of voice.

She whirled around. A small, slightly bent old man in overalls and a faded yachting cap stood on the path. He was glaring at her with such venom that she stepped back against the door.

"You related to *them?*" he barked at her.

"Who?" she said faintly. She glanced up the

street, but no one was in sight. The grocery store and the post office were closed. People had gone home to dinner.

"Them that's ruinin' the schoolhouse. You related to them?"

"I'm their daughter." She giggled, half from fear, half from the ridiculous thing she had just said. As if she had three mothers or something. But her laugh died out quickly as he came closer to her, his head thrust forward, his fist clenched.

I could leap off the steps sideways, she thought. I could outrun him. But she was too frightened to move.

He grabbed her by the arm. "You come along with me."

"No!" She braced her feet. But he was surprisingly strong for someone who looked so ancient.

"I'm gonna show you somethin', and you look at it good." He pulled her off the steps and over to the side of the schoolhouse. With a shaking, gnarled forefinger he pointed to a small gray clapboard house directly behind the schoolhouse. It was a neat little house with a vegetable garden between it and the schoolhouse, and lilac bushes against the side. "You see that house?"

"Yes." Her voice squeaked. His grip on her arm hurt. She thought about screaming, but there weren't any other houses near enough for anyone to hear her.

"That there is my home. Bought and paid for. No

49

mortgage. I worked and scraped years for that house. Went to the Grand Banks and George's Bank and fished for years in all kinds of weather, nearly lost my life any number of times. Bought that house for my wife. She died there." He shook her. "You hear what I'm saying?"

"Yes." In spite of her terror, she was curious. Why was he so angry with her?

"My wife died in that house, and I ain't-a going to give it up on no account."

"Who says you have to?"

"I know what's gonna happen. Don't try to tell me different. They're gonna make a parkin' lot right along the side of the schoolhouse and round back there where my garden is. Don't tell me different . . . I seen the plans at the Town Hall. I went to town meeting, and I told 'em and I told 'em, I ain't gonna have it. Next thing you know, they'd decide they got to take my house, bigger parkin' lot. Eminent domain. I know how those things go. Communism is what it is."

"But they can't do that."

"That's what I say, they can't do it. I ain't-a gonna let 'em, if I have to burn the place down to stop 'em."

"Oh, don't do that." In his emotion he had loosened his grip on her arm, and she took a cautious step backward. "I don't think they have any idea of doing that." She began to feel sorry for the poor old man. No wonder he was so upset.

"They say my garden's on the schoolhouse land."

"Is it?"

"I been gardenin' there for forty years, me and my wife. Possession is nine points of the law. Says so in the Bible."

"Does it really?" She knew she ought to run while she could, but now the old man interested her. Besides, a germ of an idea was growing in her mind. If the old man stopped the restaurant on legal grounds . . . Once again she had a vivid picture of herself occupying her grandmother's big airy bedroom, the house quiet, all hers, the furniture put back the way it belonged . . . "Do you have a lawyer?" she asked him.

He spat contemptuously. "Lawyers. Crooks, all of 'em. Charge you the earth, and what do you get? Nothin'."

"Well, you ought to talk to the mayor."

"Ain't any mayor here. We got a board of selectmen, bunch of fatheads. They grin and they offer me a cup of coffee . . . don't even know how to make decent coffee. Bunch of lunkheads, the lot of 'em." He looked as if he were ready to cry.

"Listen," Kelly said, "I'll tell my mother about it. I don't believe she knows about it."

He stared at her with his almost colorless eyes. "She the cap'n of that crew?"

"Well, no, but she's one of them. They don't mean any harm. They just want to be . . . you know . . . like entrepreneurs, and make some money."

"Money, hah. She'll fail, you mark my words."

Kelly wasn't sure whether 'she' meant her mother or the business. Sailors said 'she' when they meant ships and things. "I'll tell her, I really will." She backed away. "Don't worry, Mr. . . . What's your name?"

He gave her a scornful look. "Everybody knows my name." He turned away abruptly and walked off toward his house, half stumbling. She watched him stop and prop up a tomato vine in his garden.

She ran toward her grandmother's house feeling more light-hearted with every step. They would have to give up the restaurant for legal reasons, and Sarita would take her family back to her own house, which she had rented, and Nanci would find a place to rent because she and Butch had never bought a house on account of moving around so much. And she and her mother would have Grandmother's house to themselves. She would probably never get to play Mercutio, but there would be other things. Never again would she have to listen to Esther's boring stories and live in that messy room, never would she have that little creep Jeannette trailing her around, never would Alexander go crashing down the stairs just when she was trying to concentrate on a book or something. She slowed down a little. Never would she hear Jake's guitar? Maybe he would want to rent the barn room from her mother. Her face brightened again. Although he hadn't shown any signs of it whatsoever, he must kind of like having her around. He was just shy, that was all.

She ran lightly up the back steps and into the little hall where coats and boots were kept. She would tell them they would have to change their plans. Even if the old man didn't have a very airtight legal case, it would be inhumane to ruin his old age like that, and she was sure her mother and the others weren't inhumane.

To catch her breath she leaned against her grandmother's old tweed cape that still hung on a hook by the kitchen door. It smelled faintly of lavender, and for a moment she missed her grandmother so much she could hardly stand it.

The women were in the kitchen. She could hear them talking, and she could smell the baking haddock with Nanci's good red bell pepper sauce. She heard her mother say something she couldn't catch, and then Nanci spoke, close to the door where Kelly was standing.

"Well, I think it's just great the way Kelly is pitching in and helping out. It was so cute her coming up with that Blue Strawberry idea today."

Sarita spoke. "Let's don't tell her we'd already thought of it. Let's give her the credit. It's good therapy."

"Well, I don't know about that." Her mother's voice was clear now. "I don't know if it's a good idea to give her the credit for something Nanci already thought of."

"Oh, give the kid a break," Sarita said. "At that

age they need all the self-confidence they can get. That's why I encouraged Esther to take up cheerleading."

"And she did give us the idea about the blackboard and the stove," Nanci said.

"I *am* pleased that she's taking an interest." It was her mother's voice. "She was so opposed at first, I was worried. Kelly is used to having her own way."

"Only child . . . father and all . . . We'll all be supportive . . ." The voices faded as the women left the kitchen.

Kelly was so mad she sat down on a pair of old rubber boots on the cool floor. Supportive! Therapy! As if she were some kind of disturbed person. Or a baby that had to be pampered. And she'd thought they were talking to her as if she were an adult. They were traitors, even her own mother.

Angel pushed open the screen door and curled up in Kelly's lap. It was dark in the hall, and Kelly thought she might just stay there. Let them hunt for her all over town. Let them drag the river.

"I am not going to tell them about that old man," she said to Angel. "I'm going to help him." She huddled against the bottom of her grandmother's cape, feeling the rough tweed on her cheek. Angel purred and tried to wash Kelly's face.

"Don't," Kelly said.

After a while the door opened abruptly. It was Jake, and he nearly stepped on her.

"Hey!" He sounded startled. "Kelly? Is that you? I almost fell over you. What's the matter?"

It was the longest speech he had ever made to her, but she was in no frame of mind to be grateful.

"Nothing," she said. He probably thought she was a baby too, somebody you could kid along, the way a doctor says "you're looking great" to somebody who's dying of cancer.

He stood there looking down at her in the half dark. He smelled faintly of shaving lotion, and for the first time it occurred to her, with a shock, that he might have a girl friend.

"You sure you're okay?" he said. "Why are you sitting on the floor?"

"I'm thinking."

"Oh." He leaned down and scratched Angel's ear. "Well, see ya."

He went into the kitchen. Nobody cared whether she lived or died.

Chapter Six

KELLY SKIPPED DINNER, AND NO ONE QUESTIONED HER
excuse that she was tired and had a headache. "I'm
being accepted around here as the chronic invalid,"
she told Angel, who deigned to go to bed with her.

When her mother brought her a bowl of Sarita's
good clam chowder, she pretended to be asleep.

"Kelly?" her mother said, touching her shoulder.

Reluctantly Kelly opened one eye.

"You aren't sick, are you, honey? Just tired?"

"Mmm." She kept her face buried in the pillow.
Her own mother, who had connived in that deception!
She couldn't look at her.

"You worked too hard today, sweetie. Why don't
you sleep in tomorrow?"

And keep out of our way with your silly suggestions that we've already thought of anyway, Kelly thought bitterly. It was as if she were four years old, younger than that obnoxious Jeannette, and had to be babied along.

When her mother had gone, she ate the chowder, because in fact she was starving. She longed to go downstairs and get another bowl, but pride kept her where she was.

Jake, practically falling over her and not even caring. He hardly knew she existed. If she'd ever thought she was falling in love with him, she could see now that that was idiotic. Unrequited love was fine and dandy for heroines in books, but Kelly was not about to go around weeping and wailing and carrying a torch over some dumb, self-centered boy who didn't care whether she lived or died. Nobody here cared whether she lived or died. "Not even you, Angel," she said. "You're only curling up here because it's comfortable." She wished she were a cat. Cats had enough sense not to care what anybody thought. Poor Mr. Whatever-his-name-was, she knew just how he felt: all alone in the world, and people trying to steal his house and the garden his wife used to take care of. It was a cruel, cruel world.

When she heard Esther coming upstairs, she dove under the covers. Esther came in with such exaggerated caution that she tripped over something and fell heavily onto her bed. Kelly heard her muffled exclamation, and she realized with glee that whatever Esther had bumped into had hurt.

A little while later she heard Jeannette pounding up the stairs, and then a conversation between Esther and Jeannette carried on in stage whispers that were much noisier than their real voices would have been.

Esther said, "Be quiet! Can't you see Kelly's asleep?"

"I'm being quiet," Jeannette said.

"Well, go away."

"I don't have to." Here Jeannette broke into her real voice.

"Hush! If you don't go away, I'll tell Mom."

"I brought her something."

"Well, put it down beside her bed and LEAVE."

"I hate you. You're mean."

"Sometimes I hate you too. No, I don't, it's wicked to hate your sister, but hurry up and get out before I crack you over the head."

Footsteps. Kelly could hear Jeannette's heavy breathing very close to her ear. She tried to make a sound like the groan people make when they're asleep.

"She's asleep." Jeannette's whisper rasped in Kelly's ears.

"Of course she's asleep, stupid. Get out."

"If you're here, I can be here."

"This is my room. Anyway I'm going to watch TV. Come *on.*"

Kelly heard their footsteps, the pat-pat-pat of Esther's sneakers and the clump of Jeannette's oversized boots. The light clicked off. The door closed, and there was blessed silence.

Kelly lay still, thinking about her room in Wellesley, the tan carpeting that kept your feet from getting cold, the big window that let in morning light, the smallness and tidiness of the room. She sighed and turned on her bedside light. Beside her on the floor there was a dish of pudding with two bites gone.

"Yuk," she said, but it was Nanci's good caramel custard, and she was very hungry. When Angel jumped off the bed to investigate, Kelly picked up the dish. She ate the pudding and let Angel lick the dish.

Then she noticed something. Jeannette had left her one-eared tailless rabbit, Cottontail, propped up against the bed. Kelly picked it up. It was a pretty revolting creature. Jeannette had had it since she was a baby, and it was ragged and dirty. A new smear of caramel custard dimmed one of the button eyes.

"Still," Kelly said to Angel, "it's surprising she left it for me." She put the rabbit down. "She's never without it. People are surprising."

After a while the house grew quiet. She could hear the bass tones of the TV, and she knew this was Esther's night to watch Simon and Simon. She had a crush on the younger Simon. Jeannette would be in bed, and maybe Alexander too, although who could tell about Alexander. Her mother and the other

59

women would be huddled in Grandfather's library going over budgets and supply orders and other boring things. And she was starving.

Quietly she went down the back stairs to the kitchen, and without turning on the light she made herself a peanut butter and raspberry jam sandwich. She was groping in the refrigerator for milk when she heard someone coming. Hastily she grabbed the sandwich and went out the back door.

It was a warm spring night, smelling of lilacs, and the sky was soft with starlight. For a minute she looked up, wondering what was up there. Where was it that her father and her grandparents were, and did they know how discouraged she was feeling?

The faint sound of the guitar came from the barn. The insistent rhythm made her feel funny, like dancing in spite of being discouraged.

"Hsst! Kelly."

She had wandered near the fence without remembering to look out for Rhonda, and there she was, beckoning. It was impossible to turn away without being totally rude and mean, so she walked nearer and then stopped. Rhonda had changed completely. This time her hair was cut so close to her head, she almost looked scalped. She was wearing long dangly earrings that looked like tiny pineapples; three necklaces were wound around her long thin neck, and she had a fringed shawl wrapped around herself. She had on so much eye makeup, she looked like a clown.

"Hi, Rhonda," Kelly said, still staring. "You look different."

"It's my new persona," Rhonda said. "From the 20's. I'm thinking of doing a different decade every month."

Kelly couldn't think of an appropriate answer.

"That way, I'll be prepared for any part they want me to play."

"Who?"

"The TV people of course."

"You mean you're going to be an actress?"

"A star."

"I thought you wanted to get married."

Rhonda gave an airy wave. "Maybe, in my spare time."

"But you talked about having great romance and all that . . ."

"My dear Kelly." Rhonda sounded weary and aged. "A woman can change her mind. I change at least once a week. That's how people mature."

"They do?" Why am I asking these stupid questions, Kelly thought; but in spite of herself, she found Rhonda interesting. Nobody at Buckmaster had talked about being a star, unless you counted the school play.

"Your grand passion," Rhonda was saying, "your genuine *affaire de coeur,*" (she pronounced it 'core') "just happens. When you least expect it, you're swept off your feet into an agony of bliss. It might be more interesting than marriage."

"Do you still have a crush on Jake?"

Rhonda shuddered. "A crush is what children have. I shall ever love Jacob Childs DeWitt with a heart inflamed with desire, mad with ecstasy denied . . ." her voice did an interesting tremolo. ". . . till the day of my demise." Then in her natural voice, she said, "I saw the Thing again. Twice."

Kelly shivered. "You did? Are you sure, Rhonda?"

"Of course I'm sure. Are you wearing shoes?"

"Naturally."

"Well, tonight we follow it. We track it to its lair and find out once and for all what evil horrors it is perpetrating."

"Rhonda, it's probably just an old man with a bent back . . ." She thought of the old fisherman. "It might even be the man that lives behind the old schoolhouse."

"Jabez Archer? Nah. He never does anything interesting. He just complains about everything." She lifted her long leg and stepped over the broken fence. "Come on."

"Where?"

"To lie in wait. It comes along the road about this time, and tonight we solve the mystery or die trying."

"I have to go in . . ."

"No, you don't." Rhonda's long fingers grasped Kelly's arm firmly. "I've been waiting for you. Tonight's the night. I read it in my horoscope."

In spite of her better judgment, Kelly went along. She liked Rhonda's wanting to be an actress. That gave them something sort of in common. "Come, sir, your passado!" She wondered if Rhonda would be interested in a duel.

They walked across the grass to the road. Down on the Causeway, cars were turning out of the restaurant parking lots and heading home. She thought about the old man's worry over a parking lot. She would ask her mother if they really were going to use his land; if they were, she would help him fight it even if she had to go to the town hall and testify. There was such a thing as justice, after all.

Rhonda pulled her to a sudden stop. "There he is!"

"Who?" For a moment she thought Rhonda meant Mr. Archer. Then she saw what Rhonda was pointing at. On the edge of the Causeway, keeping out of the light, the strange misshapen creature they had seen before was turning off the road and down toward the boat landing. It really was an eerie-looking thing, quite short, and with that big bulging back. "Maybe it's a dwarf," she said.

"We don't have any dwarfs."

"Maybe it's a visiting dwarf."

But Rhonda was not to be diverted. "Come on, we've got to hurry. It may walk right into the river and disappear."

Kelly was torn. She wanted to solve the mystery,

but she was not eager to face that weird-looking crea-ture. "Couldn't we just watch from the road?"

Rhonda gave her a withering look, made more effective by the mascara that had left half moons on her cheeks. "I never thought Kelly MacArthur would be chicken."

That did it. Together they ran across the road and down the bank toward the river. Just before they got to the landing where half a dozen boats were tied up, they stopped and crouched in the shadows.

A strange scene took place. The Thing, as Kelly was now thinking of it, reached for the hawser of an old rowboat and pulled the boat close until they could hear it thump against the dock. Then slowly and laboriously the Thing removed its hump! Kelly heard Rhonda's gasp. They watched as the hump was low-ered into the stern of the boat and pushed under the seat. Then the Thing straightened up again and paid out the rope till the boat once more bobbed gently on the incoming tide, about six feet from the dock. The Thing turned and started up the path, directly toward them.

Chapter Seven

RHONDA GRABBED KELLY'S ARM IN A TIGHT GRIP. THE Thing was coming toward them, and in a second or two it would be near enough so they could really see it. Kelly's breathing made her chest feel tight. She reached behind her and clutched a handful of rough beach grass as if to anchor herself. The Thing had its head down.

Suddenly above them on the bank, there was a commotion. A Welsh terrier was chasing a black cat. Sand showered down on Kelly and Rhonda as the animals raced down the bank. The cat gave a wild leap, landed on Rhonda's head and bounced off again. The terrier, in wild and noisy pursuit, jumped onto Kelly's lap, ungracefully lost his balance, scrabbled desperately against Rhonda's bare legs, and was gone.

"He scratched me!" Rhonda was clutching her left leg and moaning. "I'll get rabies."

Kelly tried to shake the sand out of her hair. "Don't be silly. He didn't bite."

"A scratch is just as bad. If I don't get rabies, I'll get blood poisoning."

A different voice broke in on theirs. "What are you guys screaming about?"

Kelly reared back and looked into the face of Alexander. "We aren't screaming," she said, "and where did you come from?"

"It's a free beach," he said. He put his hands in his pockets and examined them with the intent look of a scientist peering into his microscope. "How come girls scream so much?"

"I wasn't screaming."

"Well, *she* was."

"I've lost an earring," Rhonda wailed. "Oh, lord, help me find my earring." She began digging in the sand with both hands.

"Hey, watch it," Kelly said. "You're getting sand in my face."

"Help me find it. My mother will kill me."

"Is there a reward?" Alexander said.

"Alexander, please go away," Rhonda said. Her eyeshadow had smeared some more, on the left side.

"You guys are crazy," Alexander said, and he sauntered away, whistling.

"Where did the Thing go?" Kelly remembered

suddenly what they were there for. Both of them stared at the rowboat. It rocked gently on the dark water, and there was no one in sight.

"It evaporated," Rhonda said in an awed voice. "It just went up in smoke."

"There isn't even any smoke."

"I am speaking figuringly," Rhonda said.

"Oh, let's go home," Kelly said. "My mother will have fits if she comes looking for me and I'm not there." She got to her feet brushing off the coarse sand. The seat of her shorts felt damp. "I'll probably catch a cold."

"I'll probably catch holy toledo. That earring was my mother's." Rhonda clambered to her feet, still kicking at the sand with her shoe.

"You'll never find it. If you lose something in sand, that's it."

They walked home in glum silence, but when they were nearly there, Rhonda perked up. "Anyhow we know where the Thing goes when he goes by here." She stopped short, struck by a thought. "What dopes we are! We should have searched the boat. That stupid Alexander addled my head."

"How can we search it? It's not our boat."

"We'll get a search warrant," Rhonda said grandly.

"How?"

"I'll write one."

"Oh, Rhonda." But there was something impressive about the way Rhonda disposed of obstacles.

"Why not? We'll go back to the boat right after breakfast."

"I can't."

"Why not?" Rhonda patted her spiky hair. "I was going to dye my hair red, but that can wait."

"I have business at the town hall." Until that moment Kelly hadn't realized she had decided to go to the town hall to look at the plans for the parking lot at the restaurant.

"I'll go with you."

Kelly looked at her and pictured the scene. The selectmen would never take her seriously if she had Rhonda in tow. "I have to do this alone."

"Kelly." Rhonda clapped her hand on Kelly's shoulder. "We're pals, old friends of many years, soul-mates. Whither you go, I shall go."

Oh, gosh, Kelly said to herself. What am I getting myself into? Firmly she pulled away from her soul-mate's hand. "We'll see tomorrow. G'night, Rhonda."

"Night, Kelly. Dream about butterflies." Rhonda giggled, a high whinny of amusement. "Dream about the Thing." She ran up the walk to her house.

Rhonda was really odd, Kelly thought, but she did kind of liven things up.

She got into the house quietly and found Alexander in the kitchen drinking milk straight from the container. Some of it was on his face.

"That Rhonda is weird," he said. "You better not

hang out with her or you'll get weird too." He wiped his mouth, threw the carton in the trash box and went upstairs.

Esther was sitting on her rumpled bed doing her nails a dark purple. "Where've you been?" she said.

Kelly was tempted to say "What's it to you?" but she said, "Out."

"Alexander said he saw you with Rhonda."

"So?"

Esther looked hurt. "I'm not trying to tell you what to do, but Rhonda is a weird kid."

"What do you mean?" Kelly felt defensive. Rhonda was her friend.

"Well, they're nice people and all that, but her mom works in one of those big houses in Beverly Farms and she's not home much. Her dad is dead, and she's an only child.."

"Only children are not weird."

Esther looked uncomfortable. "I didn't mean that. You aren't weird."

Kelly didn't think Esther sounded convincing. "So what's weird about Rhonda?"

"Well, look at those hair styles."

"Which ones?"

"That's what I mean. Sometimes I don't even recognize her. And the way she dresses, she just isn't with it." Esther looked as if she were sorry she'd brought it up. "She has a crush on Jake. She leaves him notes in the barn."

I wish I had the nerve to do that, Kelly thought. She pulled off her blouse and reached for her bathrobe. She would undress in the bathroom where she could have some privacy. "Rhonda is my lifelong friend," she said as she walked out.

She locked the bathroom door and stared at herself in the mirror, pulling her hair onto the top of her head and grinning so she showed all her teeth. There was nothing wrong with only children. "Rhonda and I are soulmates," she said to her reflection, "and if you don't like it, you can lump it."

Chapter Eight

KELLY GOT UP EARLY, HOPING TO GET OUT OF THE HOUSE before she got trapped, but it was no use. First Jeannette had a screaming fit because Kelly wouldn't stay and watch her gargle. Gargling was a new skill that she had acquired after much practice, and she wanted to be appreciated. She tried to explain this to Kelly with her mouth full of water, and managed to spray the front of Kelly's shirt so thoroughly that Kelly had to go and change it.

Esther had already left for school, but Alexander was in the kitchen finishing a piece of toast and at the same time fishing something out of the refrigerator. Kelly saw that it was a half head of lettuce.

"Do you eat lettuce for breakfast?"

He was so startled, he dropped the lettuce. Then he picked it up hastily, muttered something, and ran out the back door. Kelly watched from the kitchen window as he dashed across the yard to the barn and went inside. Something about the way he looked when he was running brought a strange thought to her mind. She considered it as she slapped a piece of raisin bread into the toaster.

In spite of her haste, her mother came into the kitchen as she was going out the door.

"We could use your help today," her mother called after her.

"Mmm," Kelly said and kept going.

Stationed near the road, Rhonda was waiting for her.

"Yo!" Rhonda waved frantically and came galloping toward her. In the morning light her spiky hair had a purple tint. Her lipstick was dark purple. At least, Kelly thought, she was color-coordinated, up to a point. Her orange blouse did not fit the scheme.

"You'll be late for school," Kelly said.

"I decided not to go today. I've been waiting for you for hours. Where have you been?"

Kelly ignored the question. "I have to go out to the barn for something. Wait here."

"I'm coming with you. Maybe Jake is late and we'll run into him."

"He's gone," Kelly said, although she didn't know that. She didn't want Rhonda coming to the barn

with her, soulmate or no soulmate. If what had occurred to her was true, she wasn't sure she wanted
Rhonda to know it, although she wasn't sure why.
Certainly she didn't have any reason to protect that
crowd that lived with her. They were nothing to her.
But whether she wanted Rhonda or not, Rhonda
came, jangling her bracelets and whistling through
her teeth.

As soon as they walked into the dim light of the
barn, Rhonda headed for the ladder that led to Jake's
room.

"Rhonda!" Kelly was appalled. What if he *was* up
there?

"I'll just take a peek." Rhonda's long legs disappeared, and Kelly heard her try the door.

"Shoot!" Rhonda's voice sounded muffled. "He
keeps it locked." Her tanned, mosquito-bitten legs
reappeared. "What's he afraid of anyway?"

Kelly giggled. "You."

Rhonda was not amused. "He thinks that Ashton
girl is such hot stuff. She buys her clothes at Penney's.
I know, I saw her in there."

Kelly felt embarrassed. Clothes were not a subject
she wanted to discuss with Rhonda, who obviously got
hers from her mother's attic. Kelly was not a clothes-
snob, but Rhonda's were really too much: that too-big
skirt that she wrapped around her like a gunny sack,
and that see-through orange blouse with the torn
place on the shoulder! It wasn't that they were old, it

was their freakishness. But Rhonda was her friend now, and there was no point in being critical, even in her mind.

"What are we looking for?" Rhonda was lifting an old harness from a nail on the wall and peering behind it as if there might be a secret door.

"This." Kelly opened a grain sack.

"What are you looking at that old thing for?"

Kelly reached inside and took out a head of lettuce.

"Didn't you have any breakfast or what?" Rhonda said. "If you're hungry, I can give you some bran muffins that are better than soggy old lettuce. I didn't know you folks were broke. Listen, I know what that's like, but right now my mother is getting paid regular, and I made these bran muffins with a mix, and they're really good . . ."

Without answering, Kelly heaved the sack onto her back and turned sideways to Rhonda, bending over a little.

"Kelly, are you crazy or what? You look like . . ." Rhonda stopped short. Then slowly she said, "You look like the Thing." She shook her head. "But that's impossible. You were with me."

"Somebody else could have been carrying this thing."

"Who?"

Kelly put the sack back where it had been. She rummaged inside and found two carrot tops. "Who did we see last night?"

"We saw the Thing."

"Who else?"

"Nobody else. Except Alexander."

"Right." Kelly felt pleased with herself. This must be the kind of glow Miss Marple got when she'd figured out a tough one.

"So?" Rhonda leaned against the big wheel of the broken-down surrey that had belonged to Kelly's great-grandfather.

"So Alexander is the Thing."

Rhonda stared at her. Absently she patted her hair. "Alexander? That's crazy. He's just a little kid."

"I saw him take the lettuce this morning."

"But what for? It doesn't make sense. Why would he carry an old sack down to the boat every night and stash away lettuce and stuff? It's weird. Do you think he's off his rocker?"

"All I know is, Alexander is the Thing. Come on, let's go. I want to talk to the people at the Town Hall, and then I have to show up and help at the school-house."

"Oh, bore, bore, bore," Rhonda said. "I skip school thinking we'll have a fab day, and what happens? You want to go work for your mother."

"I don't want to—I have to."

Rhonda sighed. "Then I'll have to help you, I suppose. How excruciating."

"You don't have to."

"You're my dearest friend."

They walked across the Causeway, stopping while

Rhonda called enthusiastic good mornings to a boy who was hosing down the parking lot at one of the restaurants, and to a young man just disappearing into the fish market. "Bobby Shanto," Rhonda explained, "and that one's Phil McGuire. They're two of my dearest friends."

Kelly thought about the lukewarm response Rhonda had received in both cases, and wondered about dearest friends. Maybe people here just weren't very communicative.

A steady procession of small fishing boats were heading down river. Kelly's grandfather had taken her fishing a few times, but she got so upset over the poor fish flopping around on the deck that he stopped taking her. Remembering that now, she said, "Fish have feelings."

"Oh, absolutely," Rhonda said. "Everything has feelings. I believe that. Even stones."

Kelly, who had just kicked a stone out of her path, felt vaguely guilty. "I don't know about stones."

"Absolutely, stones." She picked up a pebble and caressed it. "Poor little stone. Nobody cares but me."

She's crazy, Kelly thought. Really.

It was a longer walk to the town hall than she had realized, and by the time they got there, she was out of breath. Or maybe it was nervousness. All of a sudden she couldn't remember what she had planned to say.

"Well, come on," Rhonda said, as Kelly stopped in front of the town clerk's office. "What are we going to do anyway?"

Kelly took a deep breath. "You wait here," she said, and stepped into the clerk's office. Rhonda of course was right behind her, and she began to wish she hadn't come.

A middle aged woman smiled at them and said, "Hi there, Rhonda. How's your mother?"

"Very well, thank you," Rhonda said.

It was the first time Kelly had heard Rhonda sound unsure of herself, almost childlike, but she didn't have time to think about it.

"I'm Kelly MacArthur . . ." she began.

"Of course you are. You look like your mom. She and I were in the same grade in school. In fact I think we're some kind of third or fourth cousins. I guess everybody in town is related to everybody else one way or another."

"Oh," Kelly said. "Yes." She hadn't expected such a personal conversation. "Well, uh . . . Could I look at the plans for the parking lot and all that, at the schoolhouse?"

"Sure thing." The woman, whose name according to the neat brass plate on the counter, was Rose Burnham, went to a file cabinet and opened the second drawer. To Kelly's relief she had not asked why Kelly wanted to see the plans.

Kelly glanced at Rhonda and looked away again

as Rhonda raised her dark-penciled eyebrows in a question.

"Here we are." Mrs. Burnham brought the plans to the counter and turned them toward Kelly. "This what you want?"

Kelly nodded and squinted at the plans. She hadn't realized that it wasn't all that easy to figure them out.

"Goodness, how time flies," Mrs. Burnham was saying. "I remember so plain when Jean didn't look any older than you do. In fact, I remember her in the second grade, the time Walter Haskell painted her braids with a red marker and she didn't even know it. Boy, was she mad when she found out! She chased Walt all over the playground."

Kelly gave her a vague smile, trying to concentrate on the plans and at the same time imagine her mother in the second grade. With her finger on the paper, she said, "Is this where it goes around in back, on Mr. Archer's land?"

"B'lieve so. Jabez hasn't been giving you folks a hard time, has he?"

"Oh, no," Kelly said quickly. "It doesn't really seem fair though, does it? Using his land?"

"Well, as I understand it, there's no idea of using his land. The town let him have that space there for a garden, but that land rightly belongs to the school. If Jabez wants to make a fuss, he hasn't got a prayer. I know he's hung around here some, claiming it's his land, but it isn't."

"What about the law of possession?"

Mrs. Burnham laughed. "Jabez *has* been bugging you. There's no such thing, dear, anyway no such legal thing as possession being nine tenths of the law. Not when the deed to that land says it belongs to the school district free and clear. Listen, honey, don't you let that old coot pester you. I feel kind of sorry for him, but he's a little bit off in the upper story, always has been. Tell your mom 'hi' for me, will you? Tell her I want to get together with her and talk about old times."

"I will. Thank you very much."

When they were outside, Rhonda said "Well. What was that all about? If I'd-a known you were coming all this way just on account of old Jabez . . . I mean that old man is running on three cylinders. He's out of it, cuckoo, over the rainbow, you know what I mean?"

Kelly sighed. Her feet hurt, and now they had to walk all the way back. "I just had to find out something."

"If you'd trusted me, I could have saved you the trip. But no, you tell me you got this big secret, this plot . . ."

"I never said I had a plot."

"Listen, are we best friends or aren't we?"

Kelly considered the field of candidates for the

position of Kelly's Best Friend. She sighed again. "I guess so."

"Then we tell each other stuff from here on out, right?"

"Right."

"Now we'll go put in an hour for your mom, and then we'll investigate what's in that old boat. I should have known that was Ponty Fletcher's boat, but I was so busy trying to figure out what the Thing was, I didn't notice. Let's hurry up now so's we can get that hour over with and get this show on the road."

Kelly freed her arm from Rhonda's tight grip. "Rhonda, we may be best friends, but you don't have to *take charge.*"

Rhonda sniffed. "I always take charge. I'm an executive type."

But even Rhonda's executive abilities were not enough to overcome Sarita's.

"How nice of you to come help us out, Rhonda," Sarita said, beaming at Rhonda. "And boy, have we got work for you guys! We need to get the brush and weeds and junk cleaned out all around the building. I brought hoes and a spade. Oh, Rhonda, I'm so glad you came. It's a backbreaking job, too much for one person."

Rhonda swallowed visibly and said in a faint voice that she'd be glad to help. Kelly marvelled at the difference between the best-friend Rhonda and the public Rhonda. Maybe it was adults that intimidated her. She vaguely remembered Rhonda's mother as being on the bossy side.

Her mother was on a stepladder touching up paint above the window frames. She threw a kiss at Kelly, and Kelly felt instant guilt. If her mom knew that she had just been trying to establish Jabez Archer's claim to the land behind the school, she would not look so approving. But I believe in justice, Kelly told herself, and Mr. Archer's cause is just. In the back of her mind, however, some imp of honesty said, "Is it really Mr. Archer's cause you care about, or your own?"

She grabbed a hoe and put moral dilemmas out of her mind. Surprisingly Rhonda was a good worker. She hiked her crazy skirt up under her beaded belt and went at the weeds as if they were mortal enemies.

They worked all morning, and by noon they had cleared great piles of trash and weeds and ragged grass. For a reward Kelly's mother took everybody to lunch at the Ship Ahoy, where Rhonda ate twice as many fried clams as anyone else, and Kelly wondered about the staying power of bran muffins. It occurred to her for the first time that perhaps Rhonda wore those weird clothes because she didn't have the money to get anything else. Still, they didn't have to be quite so bizarre, did they? And all that makeup?

Rhonda flirted so frantically with the busboy that finally Nanci put her hand over Rhonda's and said, "Honey, why don't you have a nice hot fudge sundae?" Rhonda was diverted for the moment.

They went back to the schoolhouse to work some more.

"Isn't that Petey Bowers cute?" Rhonda said, referring to the busboy. "I was mad about him last year."

"Why do you care so much about boys?" Kelly said.

Rhonda looked at her as if she were crazy. "What else is there to care about? The minute I get out of school I'm going to be married, and I can hardly wait."

Kelly sighed. Rhonda had 'matured' again. "Who to?"

Rhonda leaned on her hoe and looked dreamy. "Mr. Right."

"Oh, Rhonda. What about your career? TV?"

"I can handle both."

"Who are you going to marry? Jake?"

"He'll probably look like Matt Dillon, a little."

Kelly forgot about Rhonda's love life because at that moment Mr. Archer came out of his house and stood in his garden, glaring at them. Kelly called, "Good morning, Mr. Archer," and he shook his fist at her.

"It's afternoon," Rhonda said. "And don't pay any attention to him. He's loopy."

Mr. Archer went back in the house, and about fifteen minutes later he came out carrying a sign, like a picket's sign. He began to march up and down on the edge of his garden. Kelly had a little trouble reading the crudely lettered cardboard that was tacked to what looked like a broom handle, but finally she made it out: THIEFS. COMMIES. LAND STEALERS.

"Poor Mr. Archer," she said. "I don't think it's right. I'm going to talk to my mother." She put down her hoe and went into the schoolhouse.

"Mom." She spoke to her mother's hunched-over back. Mrs. MacArthur was polishing the brass rail of the old stove.

"What, honey?" She glanced at Kelly, but she kept on polishing. Years of soot and dust were coming off the brass. "Isn't this going to be nice? I love brass."

"Mom, Mr. Archer is really upset."

"Who?"

"She means Jabez Archer," Nanci said. "He lives in the little house behind us. He thinks we're going to steal his land."

"Aren't you?" Kelly said. All the women looked at her.

"No, Kelly, of course we aren't," Nanci said. "He doesn't own that place where he gardens. His property line is on the other side of the garden."

"But he likes that garden. His wife started it."

"He's been bugging you," Sarita said.

"He just talked to me, that's all. I feel sorry for him."

Nanci put down her bottle of Windex. "In the first place, Kelly, it isn't his land, and in the second place we may never want to use it anyway. We just had to persuade the selectmen that if we needed to, we had that space for parking. They don't want people parking on the street."

"We're starting with that space next to the schoolhouse," Kelly's mother said. "That may be all we'll ever need."

"He thinks you'll take his whole place. Prominent domain."

"Eminent," her mother said. "That's nonsense. You ought to know we wouldn't drive a poor old man out of his home."

It irked Kelly that she had said 'prominent' when she knew perfectly well it was 'eminent.' They would laugh about it later. It was hard to act grownup when people expected you to make childish mistakes. "Eminent," she said, "whatever. Do you want us to clear the land right up to his garden, or what?"

"No, no, dear," Sarita said. "Just around the building. We have to keep the Board of Health happy."

"He's picketing you," Kelly said.

"What?" Nanci said, and they all stared at Kelly.

"Picketing. THIEFS. COMMIES. LAND STEALERS."

"Oh, good grief," Sarita said.

"Look, just don't pay any attention," Nanci said. "He's a little bit senile. He gets mad at everybody, especially since his wife died. I think he thinks it's the town's fault."

"Just ignore him," her mother said. "He's harmless. Isn't he?" She looked at Nanci.

"Oh, sure," Nanci said.

"Look, you and Rhonda are doing a wonderful job," Sarita said. "We'll pay you."

"No, you won't," Kelly's mother said. "Kelly is part of the family."

"Rhonda isn't," Kelly said.

"So we'll do something for Rhonda," her mother said impatiently. "Now don't bother us, Kelly, please. We're all tired, and we have a lot to do."

Kelly went outside. Mr. Archer had disappeared, and Rhonda was standing by the open window. "You were eavesdropping," Kelly said sternly.

Rhonda looked indignant. "I hope a person can rest once in a while without being accused of criminal behavior." She hacked at a clump of goldenrod. "But if they really want to pay me, I won't object. I mean, it would make them feel better. My mother says honest wages for honest work makes Jack a fine boy."

For a moment Kelly struggled with that, trying to think what the real quotation was, but she gave up. She felt disgruntled. Nobody understood her. She had persuaded herself in the last few minutes that her heart really did bleed for Mr. Archer. He might be old and senile, but they'd all be old some day, and how would they like it if somebody tore up their garden and threatened to take over their home?

"When are they going to get this show on the road?" Rhonda asked her.

"What show?"

"The restaurant, the schoolhouse, when is it going to open?"

"Oh. June 15th, if everything gets done."

"Maybe they'll need experienced help," Rhonda said. "I'm very good at shucking clams."

"They aren't going to have clams."

Rhonda looked shocked. "Not have clams? In Essex?"

"They're into fish chowder."

"*Just* fish chowder?" Rhonda sniffed. "Well, I can skin a fish."

Kelly was about to say something sharp, but the look on Rhonda's face stopped her. It was the same look she had seen at the town hall, an almost scared look, or as if she were asking for something she desperately needed. It seemed out of character, and it disconcerted Kelly. Maybe Rhonda really needed a job. Maybe she *was* scared, and that was why she acted so weird sometimes. Kelly frowned. She didn't like to have to analyze people. They ought to be simple, all of a piece, the way she was herself. "You missed that one." She pointed to a tall, thick clump of ragweed.

"I'm getting to it," Rhonda said.

At the end of the afternoon Sarita praised them extravagantly, and took Rhonda aside for a minute. Rhonda came back beaming. After the women had left, she said, "They came through." She held up a ten-dollar bill.

Kelly put away the hoes. It wasn't fair to pay Rhonda and not her. Nobody was fair in this thing. She was walking down the street, not listening to Rhonda's chatter, when she realized that she had gone off with the key in her pocket, forgetting to lock the door. She thought about going back. Her mother had scolded her the last time she forgot, the night Mr. Archer had scared her. But they were already halfway home, and she didn't want to run back. Her muscles ached from all that digging. She'd get up early and lock it before the women came back in the morning.

"Meet me tonight," Rhonda said, "same time, same station."

"What for?"

"Tonight we'll solve the riddle of the Thing."

"How?"

"Oh, Kelly, you have no imagination. We'll follow him, of course, and after he leaves, we'll examine the boat."

"Isn't that trespassing or something?"

Rhonda scorned the question. "Be there. I'll bring a flashlight."

Chapter Nine

KELLY DID NOT MEET RHONDA THAT NIGHT. IT WAS A
Friday, and the whole 'family', as they were calling
themselves now, decided to go to the local baseball
game. Kelly did not like baseball, but Jake was on the
team so maybe it would be interesting.

But it wasn't. Jake sat on the bench for the whole
game. Sarita and Nanci and Kelly's mother and the
kids cheered and yelled for the Essex team as if the fate
of the world depended on it. Kelly couldn't believe it.
Her sensible, cool mother, screaming her head off
when some guy named Arthur made a home run. What
difference did it make?

"Wasn't it a great game?" they all said to each
other afterward. They were eating fried clams at

Woodman's, and Jake wasn't even there. He was off somewhere with the guys.

"Wasn't it terrific?" Esther said to Kelly. "Isn't that Arthur Means something?"

"Which one was he?" Kelly said, and they all looked at her as if she had lost her mind.

"Kelly's not really into baseball." Her mother sounded as if she were apologizing.

"I guess I'm just unAmerican," Kelly said.

The next morning she found Rhonda waiting for her, and she wondered for a moment how many hours Rhonda spent just lying in wait. "I'm sorry about last night," Kelly said. "I had to go to that stupid game."

Rhonda brushed away the apology with a languid hand. "I was busy anyway. I had to do my nails." Her fingernails were painted bright pink and filed to sharp points.

Kelly heard the phone ringing in the house, and since no one was at home, she went back in to answer it.

It was her mother, and she sounded mad. "Kelly, do you have the key to the schoolhouse?"

"Oh. Yeah, I guess I do." She felt for it in her pocket. "I forgot."

"You also forgot to lock up. Get over here right away, please." And her mother hung up.

"I'm in trouble," Kelly said to Rhonda. "We forgot to lock up the schoolhouse yesterday. I have to go over there with the key. My mom sounded mad."

"Why should she be mad about that?" Rhonda loped along beside her. "We never lock our house."

When they got there, all three women were standing outside, and there was a police car parked in front. A man in police uniform came out of the schoolhouse.

"Oh, hey, there's Art Bascom," Rhonda said, her face lighting up. "Isn't he cute? I love him in that uniform. He's the only cop in town, and I'd love to marry him."

"What's going on?" Kelly felt nervous. Obviously something had happened, and obviously it was not something good. She went up to her mother, who looked at her coldly and held out her hand.

Kelly gave her the key. "What's the matter?"

"Go inside and look," her mother said.

"Well, we can't blame Kelly," Sarita said. "Whoever it was would probably have broken in even if the door was locked."

"It looks like kids," Art Bascom was saying. "Vandalism. They'll do it every time."

Kelly went inside, with Rhonda at her heels. At first she didn't see anything wrong. Then she looked at the north wall and gasped. Across the fresh paint that Sarita had worked so hard to put on someone had painted a large red X, and beneath it the word OUT. The red paint had run in uneven trickles down to the baseboard.

"Oh, no," Kelly said faintly. She sat down on the old paint-smeared kitchen chair in the middle of the room and stared at the wall.

"It wasn't me," Rhonda said.

"Mr. Archer?" Kelly said.

"Jabez?" Rhonda looked surprised. "Nah, he hasn't got the imagination."

When they came outside, Nanci was saying, "I just wondered if Jabez Archer . . . He doesn't want us in here, you know."

Art Bascom shook his head. "Jabez wouldn't do that. It was kids, I'd lay odds. I'll talk to some of the boys I know around town. Meanwhile, folks, keep the place locked up." He put his report pad back in his pocket and walked off to his car.

"Well," Sarita said, "we'll just have to repaint it." She was trying to sound cheerful.

"I'll do it," Kelly said. "It was me that left the place unlocked."

"Rats!" Rhonda said under her breath. But she stayed and spelled Kelly until the wall was once again a pure white. The other women worked at various jobs, but everyone seemed disheartened.

When they were finished, Kelly's mother locked up, and double-checked the window locks. Kelly headed off toward Jabez Archer's house.

"What now?" Rhonda said. "I thought we were going to check out the boat."

"First I have to find out," Kelly said.

But if there was anyone home at the Archer house, he was not answering the doorbell or the loud knocks. Kelly put her ear to the wood panel of the door and listened. She was quite sure the house was empty. "Empty houses sound empty," she said to Rhonda. "He's not there."

"Maybe he went on the lam," Rhonda said. "But you heard Art: kids did it. Doesn't he have pretty eyes?"

"Who?" Kelly said, thinking of Jabez Archer's hostile glare.

"Art Bascom of course, who else are we talking about? Come on, let's get down to the river before you say you have to go home for supper or something."

They approached the river by a roundabout route, coming up behind the little rise in the ground where the dog and cat had been fighting. Rhonda, who was in the lead, suddenly dropped to her stomach in the coarse grass. "Down!" she said.

"Why?" Kelly dropped to the ground too, feeling a bit silly. It wasn't even dark, for heaven's sake.

Rhonda wriggled on her stomach to the top of the rise. "Look down there."

Kelly looked. "It's only Alexander." But she got a strange feeling in her throat, as if she ought to holler to him to look out.

"Look again."

There was a second boat, an old outboard, anchored a few feet beyond the dory where Alexander was bent over; as Kelly watched, a figure rose from it and splashed ashore in rubber boots. It was Jabez Archer. He said something to Alexander, and the two of them hoisted a black plastic sack out of Alexander's boat and stowed it away in the outboard. Then both of them climbed into the outboard, Jabez gave the old motor a few jerks with a short piece of rope, it coughed into life, and he steered the boat out into the water, heading upriver.

"Come on!" Rhonda leaped to her feet and started running toward the beach.

"What for?" Kelly followed her, totally baffled by what she had seen.

"To follow them of course." Rhonda untied the rowboat. "Give me a hand."

"But it's not our boat."

"We're in pursuit of villains, aren't we?"

"Are we?"

"Don't be dense, Kelly. Those two are smuggling something. You saw them. It must be drugs. Cocaine or heroin or something."

The idea of Alexander smuggling drugs was too much for Kelly. "You're crazy."

Rhonda swung her long mosquito-bitten legs over the side. She sat in the seat and fitted the oars into the oarlocks. "Hurry up."

"I'm not going."

Rhonda stared in disbelief. "Not going? Are you on the side of law and order or aren't you? Do you know that every year thousands of innocent children are lured into drugs by unscrupulous dealers? Don't you want to share the reward? There's always a reward."

Well, she couldn't just stand there, could she, and let Rhonda go in pursuit of the outboard alone? She climbed into the boat and sat on the edge of the stern seat. "How do we know this boat won't sink?"

Rhonda gave her a withering look. "For an adventurer, Kelly, you are a flake. I have to do *everything.*"

"Then you can have the reward." She meant it as sarcasm, but Rhonda took her seriously.

"I wouldn't do that. You're my best friend. Share and share alike." She gave the oars such a tremendous heave that one of them flipped out of the lock and she nearly lost it. The boat slewed sharply to one side.

"Watch it!" Kelly grabbed the gunwales.

"No problem." Rhonda turned her head to look for the other boat. "Where are they?"

"Way upriver. We'll never catch up."

"Wanta bet?" Rhonda began rowing with short choppy strokes. One of the oars skittered across the surface of the river and splashed Kelly with cold water. She yelped.

"Rhonda, take it easy."

"We want that reward, don't we? What are you so nervous about?"

Kelly kept quiet for a few minutes as Rhonda made her uneven progress upriver. "Do you know where the channel is? It looks awfully shallow along here."

"Know it like the palm of my hand," Rhonda said,

and five minutes later the keel grated on sandy bottom and the boat shuddered to a stop.

"We're stuck!" Kelly swung one leg over the side of the boat. "I'm getting out of here."

"Kelly MacArthur, if you desert me now, I'll never forgive you. Push!"

"We could walk back from here, along the shore. If we keep going, we'll get right out in the ocean and we could be lost."

"We aren't going into the ocean. Don't be so chicken. Push." She was backstroking vigorously with the oars, but the boat wasn't moving.

"I ought to have my head examined," Kelly said, but she got out in the knee-deep water and pushed at the bow. For a moment nothing happened, and then the boat came free with a great sucking sound and shot into deeper water. "Wait!"

The water felt like melting ice. Her socks and shoes were sopping wet, and the bottoms of her shorts clung to her legs like icy hands. When she had pictured boating on the Essex River, it had not been like this.

"We did it!" Rhonda looked triumphant.

"We, my foot!" Kelly started to wade ashore.

"Kelly, come on." Rhonda rowed toward her. "Get in quick before I get stuck again."

Kelly hesitated. It would be a long walk home along that winding shore, and who knew whether there was even a path all the way. She climbed into the boat, dripping water all over the stern. "Let's go home."

"Kelly, we can't turn back now, just when success is within our grasp." Rhonda's purple hair stood up like small spikes all over her head. "We'll catch them with the goods."

"If they're really drug dealers, they'll murder us." Kelly tried to picture Alexander as a dangerous criminal, and again she couldn't do it.

"I'll knock out the old man with the oar, and you take care of Alexander. He's only a little kid after all; I'm doing the hard part." Rhonda was again rowing hard and erratically up the river.

Kelly wrung the water out of her shorts and took off her soaking sneakers and socks. She was shivering in spite of the sunshine. She looked up and gasped a warning as the bow of the boat grazed a neatly painted inboard riding at anchor off someone's dock.

"Oops," Rhonda said. "They ought to look where they park their putt-putt."

Alexander and Jabez Archer were not in sight. Ahead the river widened, and a small island loomed.

"Watch out for the island," Kelly said.

"Oh, I know that island. We passed it last summer, Mom and me, when we went to Ipswich with the Bennetts to see the deer."

"What deer?"

"There's that herd of deer at the Crane estate in Ipswich. It got out of hand, and they're always arguing in the paper about whether to shoot some of them or not."

"Shoot deer? Here? That's awful."

Rhonda shrugged. "It's that or let 'em starve to death. There's a bunch of little islands from here on to the ocean anyway, that's nothing new."

Mention of the ocean did nothing to reassure Kelly. She had a mental picture of their boat tossing on the seas like a tiny dot that no one would ever notice.

Rhonda looked over her shoulder, located the island, overcompensated and nearly ran into a clammer's boat on the other side. He looked up and shook his head.

In a couple of minutes Kelly said, "I see their boat!"

"Where? Where?" Rhonda slewed around in her seat and lost one of her oars. She nearly tipped the boat over as she made a wild grab for it.

Kelly plunged her arm into the cold water and caught the blade in the tips of her fingers.

"Hang on, hang on," Rhonda said. "Don't lose that oar."

"It's not me that lost it," Kelly said, gritting her teeth. The oar almost slipped away from her, but by leaning dangerously far over the side, she kept hold of it. "I can't get a good grip on it."

"I'll row closer." Using the other oar as a pole, Rhonda gave a hearty shove. Seconds later the boat was stuck on a sand bar that ended at the island.

"Well, we're stuck again." Kelly clung to the oar, but she was having trouble getting a firm enough hold to pull it into the boat. She supposed she would have to get out and push them off again anyway.

Ahead of them the outboard was pulled up on the shore of the island. Alexander and Jabez were not in sight. The island was close to the shore, and the water between island and shore was shallow, but on the river side the bottom shelved off sharply to ten or twelve feet in depth.

Cautiously Kelly climbed over the side of the boat once more, holding onto the oar. The boat tipped dangerously, and Rhonda shrieked. Kelly maneuvered the oar into the boat and gave the bow a push, but nothing happened. She tried again harder. The boat seemed to sink deeper into the mud and sand.

"I can't move it."

"Give it a real hard shove."

"What do you think I'm doing?" Kelly pushed with all her strength. "Rhonda, you'll have to help."

"I need to stay in the boat so it won't drift off."

"Rhonda!"

Rhonda sighed loudly. "Well, all right, but if we lose the boat, it's your fault."

"How do you figure that?"

Rhonda ignored the question. She moved up to the bow and put one foot in the water. "It's cold."

"No kidding." Kelly hoped the sarcasm was heavy enough to sink in.

"It'll ruin my tan."

Kelly looked at Rhonda straddling the side of the boat like a stork, one long leg in the boat, one in the water. Maybe this was adventure, but it was a long way from Mercutio. "How can the water hurt your tan?"

"My tan washes off."

"How can . . ." Kelly gave up. "Hurry up, will you? I'm freezing."

As Rhonda heaved herself out of the old dory, her foot caught on the gunwale, and slowly with a deep groan the boat pulled loose from the bottom and turned over on its side. Kelly, caught off balance, sat down abruptly in the water. Rhonda had fallen forward and now she was struggling to stand up, her clother dripping, her makeup streaking her face, her mouth open in a round "O" of dismay. The loose oar drifted downstream like a tiny raft, turning gently with the current.

Kelly began to laugh. She couldn't help it. Rhonda looked so funny, and the boat was already half full of water, and the oar was gone . . . What was there to do but laugh?

Rhonda looked at her with shock, but then her mouth twisted sideways and a moment later she was laughing too. She plopped down in the water beside Kelly, and they both laughed until their faces hurt.

Suddenly Rhonda stopped laughing and pointed.

At the same moment Kelly heard the wheezy chug-chug-chug of the outboard motor. Alexander and Jabez were heading back to town.

"Help!" Rhonda yelped, her voice lost in the noise of the motor.

Jabez at the helm didn't even glance at them. Alexander saw them, looked startled for a second, then gave them a cheerful wave and fixed his eyes again on the channel ahead of them. In no time at all the boat had disappeared around a bend in the river, and only the faint vibration of the motor was audible. Then that too faded into silence.

The river, usually so full of boats, seemed to be deserted. Rhonda and Kelly got to their feet and began to wring some of the water out of their clothes.

"We've got to turn this wreck over and bail it out," Rhonda said.

"What about the oar?"

Rhonda was looking grim now. "I'll have to paddle with the one oar. Come on." She grabbed the gunwale and heaved.

Kelly joined her. "Let's rock it," she said, after several attempts had failed.

They rocked it gently at first, trying to get enough leverage to right it. Then they began to rock harder.

"There she goes!" Rhonda yelled.

But it went the wrong way. It teetered for a moment and then fell over heavily, wrong side up.

"I can't believe it!" Kelly sank down on the overturned hull. She didn't feel like laughing now. She had a big bruise on her wrist, her arms ached, and she was cold.

Rhonda waded ashore and sat down on an old log.

"What are you doing?" Kelly said.

"I'm thinking."

"Well, think good. I'm freezing." Kelly went ashore, too, and sat down beside Rhonda.

"There goes your left shoe." Rhonda pointed at the sneaker that was drifting into deep water. As they watched, it slowly sank.

"My mother will kill me. Those were new shoes."

"And unfortunately we're going to have to walk home," Rhonda said.

"What!"

"Well, we can't right the boat. There's nobody coming along to give us a lift. We'll just have to haul the boat as far up on shore as we can and walk."

"We don't even know what they were doing on the island."

"We'll find out," Rhonda said, but she didn't sound enthusiastic.

"They were probably picking blueberries," Kelly said.

"It's too early in the season." Rhonda never got the sarcasm. "Help me pull this thing up so it won't drift off when the tide comes in."

They tugged at the heavy boat.

"Your eye makeup is all over your chin," Kelly said.

Rhonda wiped her face with her wet sleeve.

"Great. Now it's on your ear."

"Oh, Kelly, shut up." Rhonda sounded weary. "Let's start walking."

By the time they were half way home, Kelly's feet were bruised and sore, and the light breeze felt like an Arctic blast. If we had stayed in Wellesley, she thought bitterly, none of this would have happened.

"Cheer up." Rhonda's shoes were wet but intact. "Think of all the adventure you'd have missed if you hadn't moved back to Essex."

"Yeah," Kelly said. "That was what I was thinking of."

But later when she had had a hot shower and changed her clothes, Kelly couldn't help thinking it *had* been an adventure. She had never had adventures like that with any of her old friends. She couldn't imagine facing danger and drowning and blistered feet with Holly Ives. After all, she and Rhonda had been able to sit on the river bank and laugh when everything got terrible, and that was important.

Chapter Ten

KELLY TRIED TO READ ALEXANDER'S FACE AT DINNER, BUT he gave her one of his wide-eyed innocent stares and then concentrated on his food as he always did.

After dinner she followed him out into the yard. "What were you and Mr. Archer doing out on the river?"

He blinked behind his glasses. He looked, she thought, more like a dwarf college professor than a drug smuggler. "Me?" he said.

"You." She folded her arms and waited, hoping she looked like Mrs. Halcom, who always crossed her arms when she was feeling severe.

Alexander took a slingshot out of his pocket and adjusted the rubber sling. Kelly wondered if it was a threat. "Me and Jabez go upriver sometimes."

"Like every day?"

He shrugged. He picked up a flat stone and fixed it against the sling. Then he dropped it and tried another one.

"What do you take in that big sack?"

He stepped back, frowning at the slingshot as if it took all his attention. "Ain't nobody's business."

She resisted the impulse to correct his grammar. "Why do you steal lettuce and carrots and stuff?"

He looked suddenly angry and scared. "I don't steal. That's stuff they throw out, in trash cans, and at the store. Taking garbage isn't stealing."

Kelly was more curious than anything else. "But what do you want it for?"

He kicked a couple of stones. "Feed the birds," he muttered.

It began to make sense. "Birds? Hey, why didn't you say so?" She felt relieved. Alexander wasn't a drug smuggler, he was a bird feeder. "What kind of birds?" She frowned. "Wait a minute. Birds don't eat carrots. Who eats the carrots?"

He glared at her fiercely. "None of your business." He ran away toward the barn.

Angel came up behind Kelly and rubbed against her ankles. Kelly picked her up. "Well," she said. "I don't know what he got so mad about. I'm not going to hurt his old birds. I was going to tell him it was nice that he did that, he and old Mr. Archer, and maybe they should join the Audubon Society. Mrs. Halcom was an Audubon bird-watcher, and she used to tramp all over the marshes on weekends looking for birds, clapper rails and stuff."

Angel leaped out of her arms and froze near a clump of tall grass.

"It's only a grasshopper," Kelly said.

When Angel refused to be lured away, Kelly went into the house and up to her room. She felt bad about letting herself suspect Alexander of evil. That nice little boy who was just taking care of birds. It was nice of Jabez Archer, too. She would definitely go to see him tomorrow and make friends with him. People shouldn't be so suspicious.

Esther was in their room doing pushups. She sat up and pushed the hair from her perspiring forehead. "Hi." She was out of breath. "I'm getting better. I do a few more every day."

"Great," Kelly said. And then because she was feeling relieved, she decided to be friendly. "Where have all the mothers gone?"

"Back to the schoolhouse. They're trying to get ready to open on the 15th. I think they want to make sure old Jabez doesn't bust in there again, too."

"It wasn't Mr. Archer."

"How do you know?" Esther looked at Kelly so suspiciously that for a moment Kelly wondered if she suspected her.

"I just know. He's a nice man."

"Kelly, I know you're new here, but you've got weird ideas of who's nice and who isn't. I mean Jabez Archer and Rhonda Jakes are not exactly the town's most distinguished citizens."

"Why don't you like Rhonda?" Kelly demanded. "She's my best friend."

Esther looked uncomfortable. "I don't mean she isn't okay. She's a good enough kid, and her mom is a hard worker. It's just that she's a little . . . you know . . . flaky."

Kelly tried to think of some of the cutting comments Mrs. Halcom used when she was annoyed. "Well," she said, *"chacun á son gout."*

"Huh?" Esther pulled her pink sweatshirt off. "What?"

"I said one man's meat is another man's poison. Or woman's as the case may be."

"Whatever that means." Esther flopped on her bed amid the litter of clothes. "Look, Kel, I don't mean to criticize." She sat up again, her face alight with an idea. "Listen, year after next when you get to high school, I'll be a senior and I can introduce you to some really nice kids. Maybe I could help you get into cheerleading."

"Big deal," Kelly said.

"I've lived here all my life and I know people. You're a nice kid, and I want to help you."

Kelly was angry. She didn't like having her friends

criticized. She yanked off her sweater and reached for her bathrobe in the closet.

"You know what I mean?" Esther said.

"Sorry," Kelly said, "I can't hear a word when I'm changing my clothes." She stalked out of the room to the bathroom as Jeannette charged up the stairs firing a thin stream of water from a water pistol.

"Get 'em!" Jeannette yelled. "Get 'em! Pow!"

Kelly slammed and locked the bathroom door.

She stayed in there almost an hour, taking two showers and brushing her teeth several times. She ignored Esther's knock. By the time she ventured back to the bedroom, Esther was asleep on her back, her mouth open, snoring faintly. Angel was curled up at her feet. And Esther didn't even like cats.

Kelly lay awake a long time, contemplating the shambles of her life. If only there were someone she could talk to, besides Rhonda. Rhonda was a fine person and a true friend, but Rhonda was not a listener. She thought about writing to Frannie or Jill, but it seemed like light-years since she'd seen them. They were almost strangers now. She would have to explain so much before she even got to the present.

She looked at Esther's sleeping form and wished she could talk to her. But Esther was sixteen and a cheerleader; how could she possibly understand anything? Besides, she thought Kelly's friends were weird. Kelly stretched her legs till her toes touched the foot of the bed. How could anybody be expected to be an only child for years, and then suddenly have to cope with great gobs of family that weren't really her family at all? Her eyes smarted with tears.

She got out of bed and brought Angel over to her own bed. "Remember how good I was as Queen Titania?" she whispered. "Those were the days." She had heard her grandfather talk about the good old days, and now she knew what he meant.

When she woke the next morning, Esther was gone, her bed unmade and clothes strewn all over. Kelly picked up a pair of jeans and draped them over Esther's desk chair, hoping she would take the hint and knowing she wouldn't. Her eyes fell on the loose-leaf notebook that Esther used now and then as a journal, mostly to keep track of games and scores. It lay open, and there was a hasty scrawl under the date, yesterday's date.

'I guess it's hopeless,' Esther had written. 'She's about as friendly as Dracula. I've done all I can. I think I've got the Liberty memorized, front flip to cradle to chair to extension to full twist to cradle ending. I'm going to practice tomorrow.'

It took Kelly a moment to realize that it was she who was being compared to Dracula, and that the Liberty was a cheerleading routine. Dracula! And she had come up to this room last night determined to be nice. You couldn't win, not with this bunch.

Everybody had gone. She ate shredded wheat with sliced banana and drank a glass of milk, then wandered out into the yard. Today the first advertisement about the opening would be in the papers. She had no hope of their not opening on time; everything was going great. Whether the place would be a success or not was something else. Probably it would, and she would have to live forever in the same room with Esther. After the coming week, school would be out, and she couldn't even count on the days to herself. Esther was going to work in the kitchen at the restaurant, and Jake was going to be a busboy, but nobody had asked her to do anything.

She sat down on the grass and pulled a pale pink rose off the bush her grandmother had planted long ago. She began to pull off the petals one by one.

"Does he love you?" a voice behind her said.

She jumped. It was Jake, grinning at her. She felt herself blush. "What?" she said in a faint voice.

He pointed to the rose. "Loves you, loves you not."

"That's silly. Where is everybody?"

"Esther's at pep squad practice. The tryouts for first team are this week." His grin widened. "She's going to try herkies today."

Kelly didn't know what a herkie was, but she didn't want to admit it. She knew he was only talking to her because there was nobody else around, but still it was surprising, and nice. On an impulse she said, "Does Alexander really like birds?"

"Birds?" He looked blank.

Either Alexander was lying, she thought, or it's a secret. "Well, he mentioned something about birds. What kind of kid is he anyway?"

"Alex? He's a good kid. Why?"

"Would he do drugs? Like smuggle?"

He had nice dark eyebrows. At that moment they shot up in V's of surprise. "You're kidding."

"He might not realize what he's doing. Rhonda and I think he might kind of be involved. Innocently."

He hunkered down beside her. "Involved in what?"

"Does marijuana look anything like lettuce?"

"Look," he said, "maybe you better tell me what's on your mind."

Briefly she told him about their suspicions and what she considered the evidence.

She expected him to laugh, but he didn't. He studied her face for a moment. The phone in the kitchen began to ring. "Look," he said. "Marijuana doesn't look like lettuce." He glanced toward the kitchen. "I haven't got time to explain now, but be down by the old boat about . . ." He glanced at his watch. "About four o'clock. We'll break this case." He ran to the house.

She watched him. He ran smoothly, like an athlete, leaping up the steps in one jump and letting the screen door slam behind him. She could hear his voice but not what he said. She hoped he wasn't saying,

"Wait till you hear what this weird kid just told me."
Now that she had said it out loud, the story about
Alexander did sound weird. But he hadn't laughed at
her. Jake was really nice. She wouldn't mind marrying
him if she had to marry somebody. But she didn't want
to sit there thinking about that.

She got up and walked out to the barn and found
Angel looking for mice, too busy to listen to human
beings. She didn't even look up from the corner near
the rear stall where she was staring intently at a small
hole, willing the mouse to come out. Her tail swished
slowly back and forth.

Kelly sat down on an upturned nail keg and
thought about Esther and her friends going to school
on Sunday, just to practice their crazy cheerleading.
All right, so somebody had to lead cheers, but to act
as it were some kind of career?

Jake came tearing into the barn, grabbed his bike,
and took off, without seeing her. She wondered if he
was going to see what's-her-face, that girl Rhonda said
he liked. She didn't like the idea.

"Mouse!" she said sharply, and when Angel
snapped her head around, she said, "April fool," and
laughed her best, mocking Mercutio laugh. She left
the barn and wandered aimlessly toward town. She
might as well give them a hand at the restaurant, since
all the alternatives were so boring.

Officer Bascom was just driving off.

"Not again!" Kelly said to Sarita, who stood with

111

her hands on her plump hips watching the police car drive away.

"No, Art was just telling us he picked up the kids who did the vandalizing. They're from Beverly, thank goodness. I'd hate to think local kids would do that."

Thinking about what Sarita had said, Kelly realized she had never lived anywhere before where people thought of the whole town as some kind of big family. She couldn't decide whether she liked it or not. She had had so much family thrust on her already, she was pretty sure she would not want to think of belonging to the whole town. Whatever happened to rugged individualism? She was so busy thinking, she tripped over a roll of carpeting.

"Watch it," her mother said. As if she had tripped on purpose. Mothers always gave you these wonderful pieces of advice when it was too late to do any good.

She did odd jobs for the women and shared their picnic lunch of lobster rolls and Cokes, but at half past three she left quietly for her four o'clock date with Jake. It was a date, wasn't it, if you met a certain boy at a certain hour? Maybe he wouldn't even show up. Maybe he was off somewhere with that girl and wouldn't even remember he had made a date with her. What was he going to do anyway, if he did show up? She hadn't even considered that.

She checked the old rowboat and found an empty sack under the bow seat. She hoped Rhonda wouldn't show up. If she was having a date with Jake, she didn't need Rhonda. She straddled the bow of the beached boat and waited, checking her watch every two or three minutes. At ten minutes of four she decided her watch had stopped. She didn't let herself look at it for a couple of minutes. No, it hadn't stopped. It was five of. No sign of Jake. He had forgotten.

Chapter Eleven

IT WAS QUARTER PAST FOUR. DISCONSOLATELY SHE SAT down on the sand and stared at the dark water of the river. He had just been putting her on. He was laughing at her because she thought Alexander and Mr. Archer smuggled drugs. Or maybe . . . a horrible thought struck her: maybe he was in on it. The master mind. Anybody who would make an appointment and not keep it might deceive in more serious ways.

To get her mind off such a gloomy thought, she tried to imagine Esther doing her pep squad stunts. She wondered what a herkie was. Or a Liberty, for that matter. Was it really all that hard? Why did you have to go to camp to learn it? She did a couple of somersaults on the damp sand. She had never been all that good in gym, but she had beaten the other kids at Buckmaster in the standing broad jump. She had the certificate to prove it.

She tried a handstand and fell on her face. Maybe it just took practice. She tried it again. Somebody behind her said, "Way to go," and she collapsed in a heap.

Jake helped her up. "Sorry I'm late. I got held up. You ready for the great detection caper?"

She was out of breath and embarrassed. Why did Jake always see her in some kind of awkward situation, choking, falling on her face . . . "Yeah, I'm ready."

"Hop in." He pushed the boat into the water and held the bow while she scrambled in. "But you have to promise not to tell what you see. It's a secret."

"I promise."

He waded into the shallow water and climbed into the boat. "We almost lost this boat." He was looking over his shoulder as he rowed into the channel. "Lucky thing Alex spotted it stuck on a sand bank upriver. One of the oars had floated off. Don't know how it got there." He didn't look at her.

"I wonder how," she said in a weak voice.

"Folks get careless."

She concentrated on a fishing boat that was passing. She hadn't even thought about the boat after they left it near the island. Rhonda should have thought of it; the whole thing had been her idea. But in her head she could hear her mother saying, "Kelly, you are

115

irresponsible." I am not. Kelly almost said it out loud.

Jake was rowing upriver with long, steady strokes, a lot different from Rhonda's jerky splashes. He was wearing a t-shirt, and his tanned arms were muscular. It was the first time she had had a chance to look at him for any length of time, close up. He really was handsome. Rhonda should see her now! she thought. She'd turn green.

What could she say that would get him talking? She could ask about his guitar, but what should she say? You play good? He probably knew that. "What's a herkie?" she said.

He looked for a second as if he had been thinking of something else and had forgotten she was there. "Herkie? Like Esther?"

She nodded.

"I don't know exactly. Some kind of routine the cheerleaders do. I think there's a man named Herkimer who runs a cheerleading camp or something, probably named for him."

"Oh," she said. Which was not her most brilliant answer.

Again he rowed in silence, checking over his shoulder now and then for the channel markers, but more as if he did it unconsciously. She had the feeling he could follow the channel blindfolded if he had to. Jake was efficient as well as handsome.

She tried to imagine what the secret could be. Mr. Archer's boat had not been moored in its usual place. Did that mean he and Alexander were on the island?

Did they go there every day? She began to feel shivery about finding out what they were up to. Jake had said "detection;" maybe he really did think there was some kind of plot.

"That pep squad tryout," Jake said, "I guess Es is pretty excited about that."

"I guess." She didn't want to talk about Esther.

"I hope she makes the first team. She's pretty good."

Kelly wondered if he would ever think *she* did something pretty good. She wished he had seen her do Titania.

"I was going to play Mercutio at my school," she said, "only we moved here."

"Is that Romeo and Juliet?"

"Yes. Mercutio is a very important part."

"We had to read it last year. It's too bad that you didn't get to do it."

He sounded so kind, she felt like hugging him. At last, someone who understood her! She was so moved, she couldn't think of anything to say. The vision of herself in tights with a shiny silver jacket, holding her sword at a jaunty angle, filled her mind. "I would have liked the fencing part. Mercutio dies."

He grinned. "There's nothing like a good death scene."

She wasn't sure how to take that, but she would just assume that he meant it sympathetically. She swallowed. Jake was wonderful.

She was sorry when the island came into view,

sorry that the boat ride was half over, and concerned about what was going to happen next. In spite of her suspicions, she sort of liked Alexander. She would hate to see him go to jail.

The old outboard was pulled up on the island just as it had been before. Jake brought the rowboat in beside it.

"Okay," he said, "let's be quiet now."

She tried not to make the boat creak as she got out. She followed Jake through the dense marsh grass and the thick brushy growth, bending over as he was, to keep hidden. In the center of the tiny island there was a grove of scrawny trees.

Jake put out his arm and stopped her. He pointed. Ahead of them, Alexander was holding out a carrot to a small deer. Jabez Archer was strewing wilted lettuce and something that looked like cauliflower on the ground near where the deer was standing.

She heard his hoarse voice say, "Now don't eat it all at once, for gosh sake. We have to work to gitta hold of this stuff."

The deer had discovered the presence of Kelly and Jake. She was staring at them with big, unfrightened eyes. Alexander looked back to see what had caught the deer's attention.

"Oh, hi, Jake," he said calmly. Then he saw Kelly and frowned. "What'd you bring her for? She'll tell."

"I will not," Kelly said. "Tell what?"

Jabez Archer scowled at her. "She's the boss's kid.

The one that started all the trouble, her mother did."

"Come on, Jabez," Jake said. "There isn't going to be any trouble. I've told you a dozen times."

"He doesn't believe it," Alexander said. He came over to Kelly. "You going to tell?"

"Tell what?" She felt confused.

Alexander looked at Jake.

"Jabez and Alex come up here every day to feed the deer," he said. "She swam over from Crane's. There's a whole big herd over at Crane's."

"They're starvin'," Jabez said, glaring at her as if it were her fault.

"And in the paper they keep saying they'll have to shoot some of them," Alexander said. "This one, I call her Bambi, she forgot how to get back, but even if she got back, she'd go hungry. So we keep her goin'."

"And it ain't easy." Jabez dug his boot heel into the sandy soil. "She can't live on marsh grass. Ain't enough of it anyways. Can't expect a critter to go feed at some restaurant in some durned schoolhouse that belongs to other folks anyway."

"That doesn't make sense," Kelly said, but her mind was on the deer. She had never seen anything so beautiful. "Can I pat her?"

"Sure. She's pretty tame now."

"Too tame," Jabez growled. "You get tame, you're a goner."

"We don't want the 'thorities to know she's here," Alexander said. "They might get her shot."

"I'm not going to tell." Carefully Kelly approached the deer and reached out her hand. The deer's eyes were even prettier than Jake's. She stroked the white band around the nose. The deer had a short white tail.

"They can usually swim good," Alexander said, "but we think she's scared to 'cause she's going to have a baby."

Kelly was startled. "How do you know?"

"Jabez said so."

"Any fool can tell that," Jabez said. "But it's a fawn she's goin' to have, not a baby. People have babies."

"Okay, a fawn." Alexander came up to the deer and rubbed her big ears. "Then we'll have to bring twice as much food."

"She'll feed it," Jabez said.

Kelly wanted to ask if deer fed babies the way Mrs. Halcom had said people do, but she didn't like to bring it up. The whole thing seemed pretty awesome. But a fawn, that would really be something to see.

"It'll have spots," Alexander said.

"Okay," Jake said, "case solved. I've got to get back."

Kelly followed him back to the boat.

"You sure you won't tell?" Alexander caught up with her.

"Of course not."

"Don't tell Rhonda. She blabs everything."

"All right." She felt as if she were part of a wonderful secret, and it felt good. "Don't worry, I'm on your side. Can I see the fawn when it's born?"

"If you won't tell."

"I told you I won't."

"Get in," Jake said to Kelly. "I have to get back."

He sounded impatient, so Kelly took one last look at the deer, who was crunching away on a piece of lettuce, and got into the boat.

"Maybe I can help Alexander find stuff to feed them," Kelly said. "When the restaurant opens, they'll probably have lots of leftover stuff."

"It's a secret, remember?"

"I'm not going to tell. I said that ten times. But I could lurk late at night and get things out of the garbage."

He grinned. "Kelly the bag lady."

Kelly thought of Lucille Ball playing a bag lady on TV a couple of years ago, and she felt instantly heroic and charming. Things were looking up. She felt like talking some more to Jake, but he seemed preoccupied. He was rowing fast, long powerful strokes, as if he were in a hurry. "Thanks for taking me over there," she said.

He glanced at her. "No sense you and Rhonda bugging Alexander as if he was some kind of criminal."

Kelly felt foolish. "I didn't really think he was. Not really." It was Rhonda, she thought, who got me into this dumb business. And now she would have to put Rhonda off some way, because she had promised not to tell, and especially not to tell Rhonda. It wouldn't be easy.

They got back, it seemed, in half the time it had taken to reach the island.

"Thanks," she said again as he beached the boat.

He still seemed in a hurry. Over his shoulder he said, "I'm going to take Alex to see Esther's tryouts. You can come too if you want to." And he was gone before she could gather her wits to answer.

She felt wonderful. She had a date with Jake. Maybe it was only for pep squad tryouts, and maybe Alexander would be there too, but just the same it was kind of a date. Wait till Rhonda heard about that. For a moment she felt guilty because she couldn't tell Rhonda all that had happened that afternoon. They were best friends after all, and you were supposed to tell your best friend what was going on. But she had a higher trust. She had promised Jake and Alexander. She ran all the way home, calling out 'hi' to people she didn't even know, just as if this were her real home town.

Chapter Twelve

KELLY AVOIDED RHONDA. IT WASN'T EASY. LOTS OF TIMES she looked out the window to see if the coast was clear, and there was Rhonda waiting out at the end of the drive. She never did come up to the house, and that was lucky, but it got to be a nuisance trying to stay away from her. It wasn't that Kelly didn't want to see her. She was dying to see her and tell her the news, at least the part about the date with Jake. But she couldn't think how to keep from telling her about Alexander and the deer. Rhonda would be sure to want to go on with the detecting. Sooner or later, Kelly decided, she would think up some story that would satisfy Rhonda and keep her off the track, but so far she had not come up with anything that sounded reasonable.

Esther was in a state of nerves about her upcoming exhibition, and she did so much whirling and flipping and exercising that Kelly hardly dared go into the bedroom without checking it out first. Anyway, a person didn't want to get too close to someone who thought they were Dracula.

To her surprise, however, she found herself envying Esther. Everyone acted as if she were about to make her debut on Broadway or something. It seemed to Kelly that the clumsy, too talkative girl she had known was turning into some kind of remote and exotic stranger. But that's silly, she told herself, dodging one of Esther's wilder spells of pompon twirling; it's only Esther, and she still leaves her half of the room in a mess.

Kelly changed her mind about five times about what to wear to the tryouts.

"It's not all that vital, is it?" her mother said, after being asked four times what she thought about Kelly's clothes. "I mean it's just a tryout."

Kelly tried to forgive her for being heartless. She was in a dither because the restaurant was almost ready and they had invited a lot of friends to a private dinner, a trial run. All three of the women were as nervous and excited about that as Esther was about her show. Kelly wished she had something to throw herself into.

"Excuse me," Esther said, bumping into her in

the bedroom. Esther was not rude to her, but she was definitely cool. Without Rhonda and without even Esther to talk to, Kelly began to feel left out.

She decided to try making peace. "I hope your thing goes real great," she said.

Esther gave her an odd look. "My thing? Thanks a lot."

"I mean your act." When Esther didn't answer, she said, "I'm going with Jake."

"I know. You've told me five times." Esther brushed past her. "Excuse me. I have to do some exercises."

"You'll be worn out before you get there," Kelly said. She wanted to say, 'I know a secret you don't know. I know about Alexander's deer.' But she had the feeling that Esther would say, 'So what?' Esther wasn't into wildlife.

Kelly had hardly seen Jake since the trip to the island, and sometimes she had the scary feeling that he might have forgotten he'd asked her to go to the try-outs or that he might have changed his mind. There she would be, all dressed up and ready to go, and he and Alexander would drive off without her.

In the late afternoon of *the* day, she forgot about Rhonda and practically walked into her outside the house.

Rhonda pounced on her. "Where have you been? I've been looking everywhere for you. Were you sick? My mom made some chicken soup yesterday and

125

there's some left. It cures absolutely everything except broken limbs. Where have you been?"

"I wasn't sick." Why did everybody always think she was sick?

Rhonda walked along beside her, gripping her arm. "I tried to ask that Esther, but she's so hung up on her stupid gymnastics, she can't even answer a simple question. I asked Alexander, and he said you were probably out smuggling dope. Why did he say that?"

Kelly blushed. Jake must have told Alexander what she had said. Probably they were all laughing at her. That was not nice of Jake.

"Listen . . ." Rhonda lowered her voice to a conspiratorial tone. "I've been keeping an eye out, but I haven't seen the Thing for two days. Maybe they've changed their MO."

"Their what?" She wanted to get away, but Rhonda was holding her fast.

"Mode of Operation. All crooks have an MO."

"Listen," Kelly said, "don't spy on them any more. They're not crooks or anything."

Rhonda dropped her arm and stared at her. "You've gone over to the enemy. Oh, good grief, Kelly, you've turned mole."

Kelly didn't know what a mole was, but she didn't like the sound of it. "I have not," she said. "I have to go in now."

126

"You just came out." Rhonda tried to grab her again, but Kelly jerked away.

"Leave me alone. I don't want to talk to you." She hadn't meant to say that, and when she saw Rhonda's face, she felt terrible. Rhonda looked as if she were going to cry. "I mean I. . . ."

"Who cares what you mean." Rhonda's voice broke. Turning abruptly on her mother's high heels, she nearly fell. But she caught her balance and hurried off toward her house. When the heel came off one of the shoes, she jerked both of them off and ran home in her red ankle socks.

Chapter Thirteen

JAKE DIDN'T FORGET. WHEN KELLY AND ALEXANDER WERE getting into Nanci's car, Kelly saw Rhonda watching them from the porch of her house. She waved, but Rhonda didn't wave back. Kelly felt bad, but by the time they were past the town limits, she had forgotten Rhonda in her excitement over being in a car next to Jake. Alexander and Jake's guitar were in the back seat. Kelly wondered if Jake was going to play somewhere after he brought them home.

She intended to make fascinating conversation; she had practiced all day. Her first question was, "Who do you think is the neatest guitarist of the twentieth century?" But he just said "Dunno," and that stopped that conversation in its tracks. After a few more attempts, she gave up. "How's Bambi?" she said to Alexander.

"Same as she was when you saw her," Alexander said.

They were not what you would call a chatty group. Except of course for Esther. She thought about Esther, who had gone off earlier for a final practice and hamburgers somewhere with "the gang." She had said that she probably wouldn't be able to eat a thing, but Kelly doubted that. Esther ate like a horse. Like two horses. She said she had to keep up her strength. Although she didn't want to, Kelly felt envious. She wished she had a gang. She didn't even have Rhonda any more. Rhonda hadn't even waved.

Jake drove expertly into the parking lot, took out his guitar and locked up. "All right, you guys, here are the tickets. I'll see you in the stands right after. Don't go off anywhere. Just stay put." He thrust two tickets into Kelly's hand and strode off.

"Where's he going?" Kelly couldn't believe it.

"He and the guys are going to play. Come on, we'll be late."

"You mean he's not going to sit with us?"

" 'Course not. That's why he asked you. Mom wouldn't let me sit by myself, and she couldn't come on account of getting ready for the blast at the schoolhouse." He jerked her arm. "Hurry up, will you?"

Stunned, she joined the crowd that was piling into the gym. She hadn't had a date at all. She was just a convenience. Jake probably hated her. She had nothing, no date, no friends, no home of her own, nothing. Her life was in ashes.

They had good seats near the front and in the center. The gym was filling up quickly.

"There's Es," Alexander said, pointing to a group of cheerleaders who hovered near the door to the locker rooms.

Maybe it really would be fun to be a cheerleader. It was such a new idea for a moment she felt an almost painful wish to have Rhonda with her so she could talk about this.

"Yuk, she's going to speak to us," Alexander said, squirming uncomfortably in his seat as Esther ran across the floor toward them.

"Hi!" she said, vaulting over the front row of seats and coming up to them. "You got good seats, huh? I put in for them weeks ago."

Kelly stared at her. It was not the same person. It couldn't be the same Esther. This person looked like a movie star. Someone else must have done her makeup because it was perfect, a little too much, the way actors do so it will be seen out there in the audience. She looked taller, very shiny and sparkly, and extremely grownup. Kelly felt suddenly shy, as if she had just met a famous personage.

"You feel okay, Kel?" the famous personage asked her.

"Sure," Kelly said. Maybe all her life she would be

thought of as a semi-invalid because just once she had faked a headache. As her grandmother used to say, "Oh, what tangled webs we weave when first we practice to deceive."

"Go away, Es," Alexander said. "It's embarrassing."

Esther laughed. "See you later. You kids stay right here, okay? Don't wander off so Jake and I can't find you."

"Good luck," Kelly said, but so faintly she knew Esther hadn't heard her.

Before Kelly could pull herself together, she had another shock. She heard music, a quartet playing a rock version of 'Hold That Tiger.'

"That's Jake," Alexander said. He pointed to the far side of the gym where the music was coming from. "They play at the games."

I'm nobody, Kelly thought. I'm an intruder from another planet. I wish I were . . . well, not dead, because she honestly didn't wish that. She wished she were a little more like Esther, so people would come to see her perform, or like Jake, whose music people listened to.

The first group of pep squad contestants ran out onto the floor as Jake's group went into a fanfare. There were an even number of boy and girl cheerleaders, dressed alike in spangly tights and jackets. It was like going to the movies. Kelly envied them with all her heart.

Parents and friends cheered as the group went through its complicated maneuvers, dividing, subdividing, girls flying through the air and being caught deftly by the boys. It was hard to know which ones to watch, they were all so good.

Then they ran off to loud applause.

"Be right back." Alexander had slid out of his seat and was gone before she could remind him that he wasn't supposed to leave this spot. What if he didn't come back? She was responsible for him.

But he was back in a few minutes.

"Where'd you go?" she said. "You aren't supposed to . . ."

"To the men's room, where'd you think? Here comes Esther."

At first Kelly couldn't tell which one was Esther, since they were all dressed alike, but then she picked her out. Alexander began clapping and cheering.

"Clap!" he said to her, when the routines began.

"Oh," she said. She clapped more and more enthusiastically as Esther and the others went through their dazzling routines. She could hardly believe that the person she was watching was Esther, her roommate who always left things in such a mess. Now she was leaping and pirouetting and flying through the air with the neatness and precision of a circus acrobat.

When Esther did her complicated leap and somersault, landing light as a feather in the boy's arms and then dancing on her toes and twirling, Kelly was so excited, she thought she would faint. Alexander was pounding her on the knee and yelling himself hoarse. Esther was special; Esther was *exotic!* Esther Fletcher, roommate of Kelly MacArthur, flipping into the air like a colorful bird.

"Pyramid flip," Alexander bellowed in her ear. "She did it!"

The audience applauded warmly as the cheer-leaders ran off in formation, doing cartwheels.

Kelly was feeling dazed by the time the third group had finished. She wished Rhonda could have seen this. Nobody was as impressive as Esther.

There was what seemed like a long wait while the judges conferred, and Jake's band played. Then over the loud speaker system came an authoritative voice.

"Attention, please. The results of the tryouts are as follows: First squad, Audrey Fenton . . ." He paused for the cheers.

"That's Es's friend," Alexander said, as if Kelly didn't know.

". . . George Mulcahy. Myrna Betts. Frank Salvini. Esther Fletcher . . ."

Kelly didn't hear any more names. She and Alexander were hugging each other and yelling and stomping their feet. They stood up and cheered when the first squad winners ran out to take a bow.

Then it was all over; the audience had cleared out, and they were waiting for Esther and Jake. The gym looked empty and lonely. Kelly felt depressed all at once. If only she could do *something*. All she could do was Titania and maybe Mercutio, and the market for that seemed to have disappeared. She knew how Jabez Archer felt. Alone. Tomorrow she would go to see him and say something kind and understanding.

It seemed hours before Esther came, herself again in jeans and t-shirt. But the radiant glow was still around her like a halo.

"How'd I do?" she said.

"Not too bad," Alexander said.

Kelly couldn't take her eyes off Esther. "You were fantastic. Really."

Esther laughed and hugged her. "Thanks, Kel, that means a lot coming from you." It could have been sarcasm, but Kelly knew it wasn't. Esther's eyes were warm. Anyway Esther was never sarcastic. I have missed something here, Kelly thought. There is more than meets the eye. Didn't Shakespeare or somebody say that? She should have paid attention.

On the way home Alexander fell asleep in the back seat. Jake's drummer rode with them, all his equipment first having to be stowed away in the trunk. One of the cheerleaders, Audrey, came with them too; and Esther introduced Kelly as "my roommate, practically my little sister." Kelly was too pleased to mind the "little." All of them were so nice to her.

They stopped for hamburgers and malts, and Esther paid for Kelly's, just as if she really were her sister. The conversation was all about the tryouts and how this one and that one did, and what a shame it was that Esther's boyfriend Peter had to be away taking entrance exams, and how cool the whole thing had been. Kelly listened intently to every word. This was how teenagers talked. In no time at all she would be like them. It was hard to imagine.

As they drove home, she decided this had been one of the most significant nights of her life. She had to do some thinking about it.

Alexander tripped over her feet getting out of the car. She thanked Jake for taking her, and walked toward the house. Esther was still chattering with her friend, and Jake was going to take the drummer home. Kelly glanced toward Rhonda's house. Rhonda was still sitting on her front steps. Still? Had she been there all evening? Kelly wanted to go over and tell her what a wonderful night it had been, but just then Esther grabbed her hand and said, "Come on, Kel, the mosquitoes are fierce out here." And Jake drove off with Audrey and the drummer.

In the house Esther gave the mothers a total replay of the evening, with demonstrations. Kelly caught her mother smiling at her.

When she said goodnight, her mother said, "Had a good time, didn't you, honey?"

"I might go out for the cheerleading squad when I get to high school," Kelly said, trying to sound casual.

Her mother kissed her. "I'm glad you had fun."

But after she went to bed, Kelly couldn't get out of her mind the picture of Rhonda dimly lit up by the porch light, sitting there all alone with the mosquitoes.

Chapter Fourteen

THE NEXT FEW DAYS EVERYBODY WAS BUSY GETTING THE restaurant ready for the preview dinner. Even Jeannette was there, sitting on the steps hugging Cottontail and saying, "You'll probably stub your toe and drop those dishes, Kelly," or else darting around trying to be helpful and tripping people up. But as Sarita said, school was out and there wasn't anyone who could be spared to babysit.

Kelly and Esther were friends now. It wasn't just that Esther had been a star, she was also a chum. She confided things to Kelly, about Peter for instance, not in the old babbly way but as if she really wanted to tell her; and she was always bringing Kelly a Hershey bar or gum or something. Kelly felt honored, because

137

after all Esther *was* a star, and she had a million friends, who often dropped by the schoolhouse to help wash the new dishes or set up the tables or whatever needed to be done at the moment. There was a lot of excitement and gaiety, and for the first time Kelly began to think that perhaps the restaurant was not such a terrible idea after all.

When she had time, she tried to find Rhonda. She even went to her house and knocked on the door, but there was no answer. It occurred to her that she had never been in Rhonda's house, at least this year, and Rhonda had not been in hers. She worried about Rhonda, but she didn't know what to do, and most of the time she was too busy to think a lot about it.

The day before the preview dinner was especially hectic. It had rained all night, and now the sky was overcast and there was a cool wind off the sea. At least, everybody said, it would drive the mosquitoes off for a while.

Kelly was setting out salt and pepper shakers on the tables when Alexander signalled her to come outside. He looked excited.

"What?" she said.

"First the good news. Bambi's got a baby."

"Fawn," she said, but she felt excited, too. "Is it okay?"

"Of course it is. It's a girl. A she-fawn. She staggers." He was grinning broadly.

"When can I see it?"

"Maybe tomorrow. We'll see."

She started to say, "It's not *your* fawn; I can go when I want to." But then it occurred to her that in a way it *was* Alexander's fawn, and Mr. Archer's. They had kept the mother alive.

"Now the bad news." Alexander was looking thoughtful.

She felt alarmed. "Is Bambi herself okay?"

"Yes, sure. But the game warden found her."

"Oh, no! He won't shoot them, will he?"

"He promised. He promised Jabez and me he wouldn't do anything . . . now. But he says when the fawn is big enough, Bambi'll swim her back to Crane's."

"Oh, Alex." She wanted to hug him for comfort, but she knew better than to do that.

"Well, if she does, she does. The warden says you can't hang onto wild animals. It isn't good for 'em."

She tried to think what to say to make him feel better. "She probably wants to go back to her family."

"The warden says he don't think anybody's going to let folks shoot 'em, and if we can find her down to Crane's, we can keep on feedin' her, although I 'spose the other deer will horn in."

"What's the fawn's name?"

"Esther."

"Esther?"

He looked self-conscious. "Well, on account of Esther can jump so good. Deer have to jump a lot."

And on account of Esther has star quality, Kelly thought; but she knew enough not to say it. How wonderful to have a deer named for you. "Now you can tell Esther. It won't be a secret any more."

"Yes, it is too a secret. Don't you tell. It's a secret till she goes back to Crane's. Then . . ." He looked sad. "I guess she won't be my deer any more."

"She'll always be your deer, Alex."

"Horse feathers," he said, and ran off down the street.

He was right, she thought, as she walked back into the restaurant, that was a gooey thing to say and probably untrue. Bambi *might* remember Alexander though—dogs did, and cats did. That reminded her of Angel, who was home alone and maybe was lonesome.

"Mom," she said, "I'm going home for a few minutes. Be right back."

"Kelly, hold up a sec," Sarita said. "Conference. Esther, come here, dear. Nanci just made a suggestion. We're four guests short for the dinner, people who couldn't make it. Nanci suggested you kids each invite a friend."

"Super!" Esther beamed. "Peter gets back tonight." She paused. "But I ought to ask Audrey—she's my best friend."

"Well, whoever," Sarita said and went back to the kitchen.

Esther turned to Kelly. "Who are you going to ask?"

"Rhonda. She's my best friend."

"Wouldn't you like to ask Audrey?"

"No." Quickly she said, "I think Audrey is terrific, but Rhonda is my friend." She was really tempted though. It would be exciting to ask Audrey. Audrey was a junior in high school. But loyalty was loyalty. "You just don't understand Rhonda. She's really a good kid."

"Oh, I know she is," Esther said. "I didn't mean to hurt your feelings."

"You're her role model." Kelly was making it up, but it *might* be true. She wanted Esther to like Rhonda.

Esther grinned. "It doesn't show."

Kelly knew she was pleased though. She wanted to make sure Esther wasn't mad about Audrey. "If I could ask two people, I'd ask Audrey. Because she's your best friend."

Esther laughed. "If we could ask two people, I'd ask her myself." Then surprisingly she gave Kelly a quick hug. "I like having you for a roommate, Kel."

"You do?" Kelly couldn't believe it.

"At first I thought it might not work, but now I think it's great. You're almost like another sister."

Kelly was startled. If Esther thought of her as a sister, did that make Alexander and Jeannette her family, too? And did that mean Jake was her cousin? She wasn't sure she wanted that.

Esther turned to leave, but before she went she told her mother, that she was going to Gloucester later

141

with Audrey. "She's got her mom's car." She turned to Kelly. "Want to come with us, Kel?"

Kelly was startled. "What are you going to do?"

"Oh, hang around the malt shop. Gloucester's got fabulous boys. I mean awesome, really. Be here at one o'clock." And she was gone.

Kelly walked home slowly, trying to imagine herself hanging out at a malt shop with girls like Esther and Audrey, and awesome Gloucester boys. That was what teenagers did, and she was almost a teenager. Maybe she should try it out for practice. She felt flattered that Esther had asked her, although it might possibly be a bribe to get her to invite Audrey to the dinner. What if she didn't ask anyone? Then Esther could ask two people. But she didn't think Sarita would go for that.

The more she thought about it, the more she wanted to go to Gloucester. Just for the experience. After all, Esther would be there, so nothing very terrible would happen to her. Esther was her friend.

By the time she got to the house, she was feeling enthusiastic. She would comb her hair and put on a clean t-shirt. Maybe the one that had the picture of the universe on it and a little dot saying 'You are here.' People always noticed that one and laughed. It would make a good conversation piece. But what if the boys were smart and wanted to discuss quantum physics and all that stuff? Well, she would just look wise and nod in the right places. She could say things like, "Do you suppose Halley's Comet will come when it's supposed to next time?" When you didn't know what to say, you just asked questions.

Alexander was in the kitchen making one of his four-tier sandwiches. "You get to invite somebody to the dinner tomorrow," she told him. "Who are you going to ask?"

"For real?" Alexander looked interested.

"You could take Bambi."

He grinned. "I know who I'll take." He went off, stuffing huge bites of his sandwich into his mouth.

Angel was in the barn, lying on a rafter. Kelly couldn't find her at first. "Why can't you come when I call you? You could at least meow so I'd know you're safe."

Angel stared at her unblinkingly.

"Good news. Bambi's got a fawn. Named—you won't believe this—'Esther.' I wish I had a brother that would name a fawn Kelly. Fat chance. If I had one and he named anything for me, he'd probably call it Dracula. Or Creep." She tried to lure Angel down, but Angel didn't move. "Guess what. I'm going to Gloucester with Esther and Audrey to drink malts and see fabulous boys. Am I lucky or am I lucky!"

She went into the house and washed up and changed her shirt. She studied her face in the mirror while she combed her hair. "I look excited," she told herself. "This is a big day, so naturally I'm excited. In sixty-nine days I'll be in 8th grade, and today I'm going out with high school kids." She wished she could tell somebody about all these things. She wished she could tell Rhonda. Holly Ives would certainly be impressed. She really wished she could tell Rhonda though. She imagined Rhonda's screech of enthusiasm. Rhonda would be glad for her. That was how friends were.

She looked out the window toward Rhonda's house. There was a light on in one of the downstairs rooms. She had twenty minutes before one o'clock; maybe she would just dash over there and tell Rhonda the news and make a date to talk later.

It seemed like such a good idea, she slid all the way down the bannister of the staircase. If Alexander was allowed to do it, she could too, even if it was childish.

She ran across the grass to Rhonda's house and rang the doorbell. She heard the whirr of the bell, but nothing happened. This time she was sure Rhonda was in there.

For a moment she thought, 'Well, if she doesn't want to see me, the heck with her.' But then she remembered Rhonda sitting on the steps in the dark with all the mosquitoes while Kelly was off having a wonderful time and being with Esther's friends. She knocked on the door. No one came. She thought about trying the knob, but if it was unlocked and she opened it, that would be illegal. She knocked again, harder and longer.

After a long pause she saw the door opening, slowly and not very far. In the dimness of the hall Rhonda looked like a ghost.

"Hi," Kelly said.

Rhonda looked as if she had been sick. She had dyed her hair black, and she was wearing an old torn green bathrobe wrapped like a cape around her.

"Look," Kelly said, "they're having this practice dinner at the restaurant tomorrow night, and we kids get to ask one person each. You want to go?" That was not what she had meant to say at all.

The door opened a little wider, and Rhonda stood back.

Kelly stepped inside, and Rhonda closed the door. It was dark and musty in the hall. "Could we go outside?" Kelly said.

"Why did you ask me?" Rhonda's voice was dull.

Kelly could see that she had on her old shorts and a boy's shirt under the bathrobe. She wished Rhonda would take off the bathrobe; it made her look like a big green bat. "Because I wanted to," she said. "You're my best friend, aren't you?"

Rhonda stared at her. She didn't have her glasses on, and her eyes looked different, kind of unfocused. Her expression was blank, like Angel's. "How can you say that?"

"Say what?"

"That I'm your best friend. You go gallivanting off in a boat with the man I love, never telling me word one. You go to some stupid tryout as if you were Cinderella, with never a clue to me. And you come home with strangers, and what do you do? You wave at me. Just who do you think you are, the Queen of England?"

"Rhonda, look. I went with Jake in the boat for a reason. I couldn't tell you because it's a secret . . ."

"I think you've joined the ring."

"What ring?"

"The smugglers. You're probably the go-between."

"Come on, Rhonda! There isn't any ring. And I didn't go to the tryouts with strangers; I went to baby-sit Alexander. But Rhonda . . ." The things she had been longing to tell her began to tumble out. "It was wonderful. Esther made first team, and she was really awesome. And she's been so nice to me lately. You'd really like her."

"I've known Esther Fletcher all my life."

"But the real Esther . . ."

"There's only one Esther." Rhonda looked glum.

There wasn't, though; that was the point. "How come you don't like her?"

"Who said I didn't like her? You were the one that didn't like her."

"Well, I like her now. I *admire* her. I'm going to Gloucester with her and Audrey in a few minutes. We're going to the malt shop in Gloucester and talk to boys."

146

Rhonda gave a little shriek, but it was not delight. "When I come back, I'll tell you all about it."

Rhonda grabbed her shoulders hard enough to hurt. "I want to know the secret. About the island."

"I can't tell you yet. Maybe later."

Rhonda shook her. She looked fierce. "Tell."

"Rhonda, I promised. Let go. That hurts."

"Tell me."

"I can't." She felt a little scared. Rhonda looked so strange.

"Did you swear it on the Bible?"

"Of course not. Ouch!"

"Did you mingle your blood?"

"No. Rhonda, let go. I have to meet Esther."

"Then it's not a real promise."

"It is too, and I'm not going to break it." Almost before Kelly could finish the sentence, she was shoved hard into the big closet near the front door, and the closet door slammed shut.

It was inky black in the closet, and it smelled funny. She was frightened. She tried to open the door, but it was being held shut on the other side. She threw all her weight against it. "Let me out!" Her voice sounded muffled. A person could die in a closet like this. The air would be all gone. Her heart pounded. "Rhonda, let me out." She fought back a coat on a hanger that seemed to wrap itself around her.

"Tell me the secret." Rhonda sounded far away.

Kelly's chest felt as if a huge bandage were being

pulled tighter and tighter around it. She tried not to cry. "I'll die in here."

"Tell me the secret, and I'll let you out."

"Esther will be looking for me."

"All you care about now is Esther, Esther, Esther. You were my best friend and you've betrayed me. All those kids with their spangles and batons and their boyfriends and their bangles and beads. They're not that terrific. It's all a lot of bilgewater. I might have known you'd betray me for people like that."

Kelly took a deep shaky breath. "I haven't betrayed you . . ."

Rhonda was pounding her fists on the door. "Tell me the secret."

If she stayed here, she'd die. The secret was going to be out soon anyway, now that the warden knew. "All right," she said, "are you listening?"

"I'm listening."

Kelly felt terrible. She didn't like to break promises. "Well," she said. "The reason Alexander and Mr. Archer go to the island is to feed a deer . . ."

"What!" Rhonda's voice as a shriek of disbelief.

"Honest. Jake took me to see her. She's named Bambi, and she just had a fawn. Now let me out."

There was a long silence.

"Rhonda! You promised!"

No answer.

She pushed at the door, and it opened. Rhonda wasn't there.

Chapter Fifteen

KELLY WAS SHAKING. SHE HAD BEEN SCARED IN THAT stupid closet; it made her mad to be frightened like that. And where did Rhonda get off treating her that way? Best friend, baloney.

She looked at her watch. She'd have to run to get to the restaurant before Esther and Audrey left for Gloucester. If Rhonda had made her miss all that, she'd really be mad. What had come over Rhonda anyway to act like such a maniac? She hadn't even said she'd go to the dinner. Well, maybe Kelly would ask somebody else. Audrey, for instance.

She calmed down some as she walked up the street. The early afternoon light was shining on the flat marshes that stretched out to sea. Rhonda was nowhere in sight. I don't care where she is, Kelly told herself. I don't want to see her ever again. But even as she thought that, she was hoping they would make up. No one was so much fun to tell things to as Rhonda. She made everything so dramatic. Yeah, like slamming her best friend into a closet and not letting her out! But in spite of herself she began to grin. Life was never *dull* around Rhonda.

Audrey's car was pulling up in front of the restaurant as Kelly got there.

"Hi," Audrey called. "Tell Es I'm here, will you?"

"Be right out." Kelly ran into the restaurant. "Where's Esther?"

"In the ladies' room," Sarita said. She had gloves on and she was giving the brass rail of the stove a final polish.

Kelly started toward the rest rooms, but Alexander came running in the back door looking upset. He grabbed Kelly by the wrist.

"Come outside. I gotta tell you."

"I have to let Esther know Audrey's here . . ."

"Never mind Esther. Have you seen Rhonda?"

Kelly was surprised. "Yes. Why?"

"What's she doing going off in our boat?"

Kelly clapped her hand to her head. "Oh, no!"

"Did you tell her the secret?" He shook her arm. "Did you?"

"I couldn't help it. She . . ."

"You promised!" He looked as if he were going to cry.

150

"She wouldn't hurt the deer." But a terrible doubt seized her. Rhonda was so upset, what might she do? Why would she be going out in the boat alone? It wasn't even her boat. "We'd better find Mr. Archer." She grabbed Alexander's hand, and they ran toward Jabez Archer's little house. Out on the street Audrey was blowing her horn. They would go without her. Oh, blast Rhonda!

It took a few minutes to put Jabez into the picture. He had been taking a nap and he came awake slowly, shaking his head and scowling and muttering. When he finally understood what they were telling him, he slapped his horny fisherman's hand onto his knee and said, "Consarn! Let's go git 'er."

Kelly tripped over a lobster pot near the door and almost fell as she hurried to keep up with Jabez and Alexander. She was very worried, about the deer and about Rhonda. She couldn't believe Rhonda would hurt the fawn, but she could cause a commotion; no one was better at causing a commotion. If people knew about the fawn and came flocking to see it, all kinds of bad things could happen. They might take it off to a zoo, or it might accidentally die, or something awful; and it would be Kelly's fault. She wished she had stayed in that gruesome closet forever before she gave the secret away.

For a few minutes it looked as if Jabez's motor wasn't going to start. It sputtered and died, sputtered and died. Then as Alexander hovered behind him, looking desperate, the old motor choked, gasped, stuttered, and kept going. Jabez backed into the channel with a wide, practiced sweep, and pointed the bow toward the island.

Kelly sat on the edge of the seat almost holding her breath. She felt so sorry for Alexander, who was hunched in the bow of the boat, his feet wrapped around a tangle of fishing gear. He looked pale, and his shoulders tensed forward as if he were trying to urge the boat to go faster.

Remembering how Rhonda rowed, Kelly didn't think she could have been very far ahead of them. Maybe she wouldn't make it at all; she might get hung up on a sandbar, the way she had before. Thinking about that made Kelly feel a little better, but not much. In her mind she kept seeing the deer and imagining the little spotted fawn close up against her. Rhonda in that wild bathrobe that she probably hadn't stopped to take off would scare any little fawn half to death.

Alexander was shading his eyes with his hand, trying to see ahead on the river. He frowned impatiently when other boats passed them and momentarily blocked his vision. The sun on the water dazzled the eyes. Kelly wished she had her sunglasses.

They passed the place where Rhonda and Kelly had gotten stuck the first time. The island was almost in sight now, a small dot in the shallows. Alexander and Kelly both strained forward to see.

Suddenly Alexander yelled, "There she is!" He stood up, and for a minute Kelly couldn't see past him.

She started to stand up too, but Jabez scowled and yelled at them to sit down. Alexander hunkered down, but he didn't really sit.

As they came closer, they could clearly see the old rowboat pulled up onto the shore carelessly, the oars hanging in the locks. Typical Rhonda, Kelly thought. Her heart was beating fast. What could Rhonda be doing? She was scared to think.

"There she is!" Alexander pounded the gunwales with his fists.

Rhonda came into view, her arms spread so that she looked like a huge bat.

"She's got the fawn!" Alexander said. "Hurry up, Jabez!"

Jabez gave a loud grunt and tried to speed up the boat, but it was going as fast as it could. It seemed to Kelly that they were hardly moving.

Rhonda was trying to get the fawn into the boat. The water was up to her knees as she pushed off and struggled to get both herself and the fawn in. Bambi was close behind them, nuzzling at Rhonda's back. Rhonda slipped, and for a moment all they could see of her was one floating wing of the old bathrobe, and the fawn's legs. She made it to her feet and tried again. This time she heaved the fawn into the stern and thrust her own long legs over the gunwale. The mother deer was pawing at the boat.

"Rhonda!" Kelly knew Rhonda couldn't hear her over the distance and the motor, but she had to yell.

"Rhonda, wait!" She couldn't tell whether Rhonda had recognized them or not.

The boat almost tipped over as Bambi tried to climb in. Rhonda grabbed one oar and used it as a pole to shove the boat into deeper water. The fawn was lying still in the stern.

"Don't let her be dead." Kelly realized she had said it aloud.

"Hurry up!" Alexander pleaded. "Jabez, hurry up."

"Got 'er up to top speed," Jabez said. He aimed his boat directly at the rowboat.

Rhonda was heading away from them, toward the sea, and she had begun to row. Bambi was swimming in the water alongside the boat. The fawn suddenly struggled to its feet, aware of her mother.

Rhonda's oar hit the surface of the water with a splash, she almost fell over backward, and at the same moment Bambi pushed against the bow. The boat spun in a half circle. The fawn fell into the water, and Bambi veered off to rescue her. Rhonda leaned over the side of the boat, caught the flapping bathrobe in the oarlock, and fell overboard. The boat bobbed sideways in the current.

As soon as Jabez cut the motor, both Kelly and Alexander were over the side. The water was cold and salty in Kelly's mouth. She saw Alexander catch up with the two deer and maneuver them back toward the island. She grabbed at Rhonda as she surfaced, chok-

154

ing. Rhonda tried to wrap her arms around Kelly's neck, and for a minute Kelly was busy trying to avoid getting dragged under herself.

She got an arm around Rhonda, from the back so that Rhonda couldn't grab her, but Rhonda swept an arm backward and hit Kelly in the face. She let go, and both of them sank.

When she surfaced again, she couldn't find Rhonda for a few seconds. She wanted to panic, to scream, to swim to shore and get out of this numbing cold water, but then she saw Rhonda again, arms flailing.

Just as she caught hold of one of those long arms, a rope end landed in the water close enough so she could grab it. She hung onto Rhonda with one hand and the rope with the other. Rhonda wasn't fighting her now. In fact, Kelly was afraid she was unconscious, she seemed so limp. But someone was pulling the other end of the rope, and they were moving toward the island quite quickly.

Even when her feet scraped bottom, she was too exhausted to stand up, especially with Rhonda's weight. She just hung on.

Rhonda was lifted away from her, and Kelly flopped face down on the rough grassy shore of the island, shivering and trying to breathe normally. After a minute she sat up. Rhonda was hunched over, near her, head between her knees, coughing up salt water. Jabez bent over her, and every now and then gave her a hearty clap on the back. Behind them Alexander was carefully mopping off and rubbing down the fawn with his t-shirt.

Jabez straightened up and wiped his hands on his pants. "All a-board," he said in his croaky voice. Ungently he hauled Rhonda to her feet and pushed her into the boat.

Alexander gave Bambi a final reassuring pat and came after them. Nobody even looked at Kelly. She got up unsteadily, wringing the water out of her shorts. I saved Rhonda's life, she thought—almost—anyway, and nobody even cares. Stiffly she climbed into the boat as Jabez pushed off. Rhonda sagged in the bow, her back toward them. Kelly tried to summon up all the anger she had felt before, but she was too tired, and Rhonda looked too despairing. What had she thought she was doing anyway? Maybe she really and truly was crazy. Somebody ought to look after her before she got into real trouble.

Nobody spoke on the trip back, which seemed to go much faster than the trip out. Alexander jumped out and helped Jabez with the boat. He did not pay any attention to Rhonda and Kelly; it was as if they were not there at all.

Still shivering, Kelly climbed out into the shallow water. Rhonda hadn't moved. "Come on, Rhonda," she said, but Rhonda still sat, her head on her chest and her face stiff.

Alexander and Jabez moored the boat, covered

the motor with a tarpaulin, and Jabez stalked off without a backward glance. Alexander looked at Kelly. "Get her out of there," he said, and then he ran off after Jabez.

"Come on, Rhonda," Kelly said. "Get out." She was beginning to get mad all over again. Rhonda was acting as if she were deaf or frozen, but she didn't move; she wasn't even shivering. "Rhonda, come on, you better go home and get some dry clothes on." Kelly waited. Rhonda sat like one of those carved wooden women on the bows of old ships. Only those women didn't have punk haircuts. "Rhonda!" She grabbed Rhonda's limp arm and shook it. "Move." She was standing in knee-deep water and she was cold. Rhonda lifted her head slowly and looked at Kelly. She looked so completely miserable, Kelly felt awful. But she was still mad.

"Why did you do such a crazy thing?"

Big tears began to fall down Rhonda's face. In a flat voice she said, "I thought if you were going to betray me, I'd betray you. All I could think of was taking that fawn back to Crane's, so there wouldn't be any Plot any more, and you wouldn't get into it and leave me out."

For a minute Kelly didn't know what to say. How could you stay mad at somebody who was so sad and goofed up? "Rhonda, there wasn't any plot. Jake took me to see the deer so you and I would quit bugging Alexander and thinking there *was* a plot."

"There was a secret, and you shut me out."

"I promised. I had to promise, because they didn't want people to find the deer and the fawn and take them away or shoot them or something."

Slowly Rhonda stood up. The boat rocked, and she almost lost her balance, but she made no move to steady herself. Kelly held onto the bow. "Come on, get out."

As if she were a hundred years old, Rhonda climbed out of the boat and walked ashore. Kelly followed her. They began to walk down the road toward their houses, both of them soaking wet. Rhonda made a motion as if to pull the old green bathrobe around her and then realized it was gone. Automatically she said, "I lost my mother's bathrobe. She'll kill me."

"She's not going to kill you for an old torn bathrobe."

"You don't know my mother."

They went on in silence. A couple of people looked at them curiously, but Kelly hardly noticed them. She felt weird.

At Kelly's front yard, Rhonda stopped. "I guess that wasn't a very good thing to do."

"I guess it wasn't."

"I just thought you weren't my friend any more, and I didn't care what I did; I just wanted to do *something.*" She turned away. "I guess I really blew it."

Kelly watched her for a moment. Then she said, "Hey, Rhonda?"

158

"Yeah?"

"You want to go to the preview dinner?"

Very slowly Rhonda's expression changed. "What are they going to have?"

"Chicken with chutney and honey. Eggplant curry. Salad with cut-up stuffed olives."

Rhonda's nostrils quivered slightly. "What's for dessert?"

"Lemon mousse with blueberries."

Rhonda took a long breath. "I'll come."

Chapter Sixteen

KELLY COULDN'T GET OVER HOW DIFFERENT THE OLD schoolhouse looked, with shaded lights on the tables, white tablecloths and real napkins, vases of flowers on the old iron stove, and people standing around sipping wine and talking and smiling. It was really the people that made the big difference. They looked so friendly. Everybody smiled at her and talked to her and asked her how she liked the town. They spoke nicely to Rhonda too, who was unusually subdued in a slightly faded blue denim skirt and white blouse. Not to be too un-Rhonda, though, she had done a crooked streak of silver through her spiky black hair.

Jake was there, looking dressed up in his white cords and a blue shirt with the sleeves rolled halfway up his forearms like a movie actor. Kelly looked sharply at his girl, but she had trouble finding anything wrong with her. She was really pretty; and when Jake introduced her, she said, "Oh, I've heard a lot of good things about you, Kelly." Her name was Janice.

"You have?" Kelly felt a little suspicious. She wanted to say, "Like what? Like I thought Alexander was a drug smuggler, ha ha?"

But then Janice said, "Jake told me you're interested in acting."

"He did?" She heard herself and wondered how she had ever gotten an A in Mrs. Halcom's Social Conversation class.

"I'm in the drama society," Janice was saying. She was looking more and more like Brooke Shields.

"That's nice," Kelly said faintly.

"When you get into high, look me up. We can always use new talent." Janice gave her a little wave as if they were old buddies.

"It won't be till year after next."

"I won't forget," Janice said as she and Jake walked away.

"Did you hear that?" Kelly was saying to Rhonda, but Rhonda was disentangling herself from the lasso that Jeannette had wound around her ankles.

Sarita came up to them and said, "Rhonda, so glad to see you. I've been wanting to ask you if you'll have any free time this summer."

"I've got it now. School's out," Rhonda said.

161

"We thought you might work for us part-time. Are you a good clam-shucker?"

Rhonda's mouth fell open. "Fabulous. Faster than the speed of light. But I thought you weren't going to have fried clams."

"We aren't, but we'll have Nanci's clam chowder every week. And there'll be other jobs." Sarita put her arm around Kelly's shoulders. "We've got jobs lined up for Kelly, too."

Kelly was surprised at how pleased she felt.

As Sarita went to greet newcomers, Rhonda said, "I can't believe it. A job! Wait till I tell my mom."

Esther came over and said pleasantly, "Hi there, Rhonda. How ya doin'?"

Rhonda swallowed. Suddenly she had that shy look again. "Good. Great. Congratulations on the pep squad thing."

Esther looked at her a second and then said, "Come over some time and I'll show you some of the routines."

"Honest?" Rhonda looked overcome. Peter came to claim Esther, and Rhonda said to Kelly, "I can't believe it."

"Well, you're my best friend, aren't you? You've heard about networking, haven't you?"

"Wow," Rhonda said weakly. "Esther Fletcher!"

"I know," Kelly said. "She seems like a whole new person." Or maybe, she thought, there was a person there all the time that I wasn't looking at.

Several people came up to Kelly and smiled at her and told her they were her near-neighbors, or sometimes they were her third or fourth cousins. Everybody was so nice to her. She had never seen anything like it.

People were sitting down at the tables, and Nanci and Sarita and Kelly's mother were in and out of the kitchen. Tonight this special feast was for friends, and the three women were going to be the waitresses.

Kelly caught up with her mother. "Want me to help?"

"Not tonight, honey. Tonight you're a guest. Tomorrow we put you to work."

The front door opened, and people glanced up to see who was coming. Alexander stood there, hair combed, face washed, clean jeans. His glasses shone in the light. "Hi," he said to no one in particular. "Me and my guest are here."

A figure that had been hidden behind him shuffled into view.

"It's Mr. Archer!" Kelly said.

"Oh, good," her mother said. "I'm so pleased he came."

Sarita crossed the room and gave him a firm handshake. "Jabez, we're so glad you came. Haven't seen enough of you around lately. Alexander, make him comfortable. How about that table where Rhonda and Kelly are going to sit?"

Jabez Archer stood with his head lowered, glaring

around the room like a small bull in a bullring. Kelly almost expected him to paw the ground. He was wearing a clean shirt and a tie, but the same baggy pants. In a loud voice he said, "He dragged me here." He gestured toward Alexander. "Said you ain't going to steal my land."

"Of course we're not." Sarita gave him a firm pat. "You know me too well for that, Jabez. Land sakes, I've known you and Myrtle all my life."

Nanci joined them and said, "Welcome to our party, Mr. Archer." She took his arm and steered him toward the table.

Alexander looked at Rhonda and said out of the corner of his mouth, "I'm not going to sit with her."

"Alex, she's sorry," Kelly said. "She didn't mean any harm to the deer. Honest."

Rhonda strolled over to Alexander, looking around the room airily as if other things commanded her attention. "Why, hello, Alexander," she said, like a TV hostess. "Good evening, Mr. Archer." With a swift underhanded motion she shoved half a dollar into Alexander's hand, and said in a low conspiratorial voice, "Buy some lettuce for the deer. My compliments." Then in her hostess voice she said, "Isn't it a lovely party, Mr. Archer? Here, let me help you with your chair."

Jabez scowled nearsightedly at her. "I could swear I seen you somewheres before."

"Probably in the post office." She pulled out his chair.

He examined it carefully before he sat down.

Alexander sat down. "When do we eat?" he said.

Nanci and Kelly's mother began bringing in the bowls of chowder, and Sarita brought big salad bowls to every table. Alexander dove into his food at once, forgetting everything else. Jabez poked through his salad suspiciously before he ventured a mouthful.

Across the room Esther was talking happily to Peter; but when she looked up and caught Kelly's eye, she gave her a warm smile. That's my big sister, Kelly thought. In a way. And Alexander was her kid brother. She looked at Jake. She wasn't ready to claim him as a cousin yet. He was too handsome to be a cousin. But that was a nice girl he had. Everybody was being nice. A woman at the next table leaned over to ask how she was getting along. "You're the spitting image of your mom at that age," the woman said.

Kelly felt strange, almost as if she had come home after a long, long time away.

"Good chowder," Rhonda said, "but maybe a tad more salt."

The whole meal was wonderful. The chicken and eggplant were both just right; the baked potatoes had sour cream and chives; the tiny rolls Nanci had made melted in your mouth. And the dessert was fantastic.

"How is the little fawn, Mr. Archer?" Rhonda said, as if she were inquiring about a new baby.

He didn't answer, and Kelly thought maybe he hadn't heard. "Is the fawn okay, Mr. Archer?"

He looked at Kelly, and she realized that she had never looked into his eyes before when they weren't angry. They were light blue, like sea water on a winter's day. "Real perky," he said. "Soon's she gets used to the world, she's gonna do just fine."

Kelly helped clear away the dishes while people lingered over their coffee. Her mother came over to her and put her arm around her. Kelly thought she had never seen her look so happy since Dad died.

"Well," her mother said, "what do you think?"

Kelly had to smile back when her mother looked like that. "I guess," she said, "it may not be so bad after all."